I0547259

BAD HABIT

A Novel

BY

BLU DANIELS

Bad Habit
Copyright © 2015 by Blu Daniels
All Rights Reserved

This story is a work of fiction. Names, characters, places, incidents and events are either products of the author's imagination or used fictitiously. Any resemblance to actual persons living or dead, places, events or locations is entirely coincidental.

No part of this eBook may be reproduced, stored in a retrieval system or transmitted in any form or by any means, without the prior written permission of the author/publisher, except in the case of brief quotations for the purpose of writing critical articles or reviews.

Chapter 1

"No! And you can't make me!"

"Alexandria, for the last time, get out of the damn car!"

"No!" she shouted, sounding more like a bratty toddler than the mother of four. I held the door open while she glued herself to the seat, crossing her arms in ridiculous protest. She wouldn't even look at me.

"Alexandria… Get. Out. The. Car. Right. Now," I hissed, gripping the door. There was a slight hesitation in her eyes. After a few moments frozen like a statue, she slowly came back to life. Unbuckling her seat belt, she stormed out the car with a huff, slammed the door shut and stumbled before catching herself, glancing to see if I noticed.

Always the graceful one.

We were parked outside the Atlanta Superior Courthouse on a blistering afternoon. The sun was just starting to set on my patience, the patience I reserved for days I had to deal with this stubborn bitch. I rubbed my throbbing temple that only beats around her. Every gray hair I have on my body at my young age, I hold Alex personally responsible for.

"I can't believe you're making me do this," she growled under her breath. "Look at me, I look a mess!"

She had on baggy jeans, a stained stretched out v-neck top, and the crusty sneakers she wore when running errands, which we had just completed. Her face was bare and her long, black hair was pulled back in a sloppy bun. I shrugged, pretending not to care.

"We have to. Now, let's go." I headed towards the main stairs, fully expecting her to follow but found myself walking alone.

Damn this woman!

She avoided my glare, holding her stubborn pout as I charged back. But the way she jumped and widened her eyes said it all. She was scared, as she should have been. She was wasting my time with her headstrong bullshit.

"What is it now, Alexandria?"

She shook her head, fuming. "No dress. No reception. No cake. No wedding. No RING!"

I loosened the tie stifling my neck and I kept a level tone. Yelling wouldn't get me anywhere, especially with her.

Rule #6: Never raise your voice. The loudest one in the room is the dumbest.

"Well, we won't be able to afford any of that if I continue paying your medical bills out of pocket."

"This is fucking nuts! I won't do it and you can't make me," she screamed, stomping her foot down, drawing attention to her tantrum. I rolled my eyes and glanced down at my watch. It was five thirty.

He'll be leaving soon.

"Fine," I grumbled.

"Fine," she snapped, narrowing her eyes at me as she opened the car door.

Not so fast!

With one swift move, I seized her forearm, spun her around, and threw her over my shoulder, caveman style.

"Ahhh... put me down, you bastard!"

She kicked and wiggled but it was like one of the kids trying to fight their way out of my hold. I marched up the stairs of the courthouse with little effort. A year ago, this feat would have been impossible. They said Alexandria weighed close to two hundred pounds during her last trimester. But she lost most of the baby weight within six months without even trying. Being responsible for four infants, you tend to forget to feed yourself.

"Braxton, put me down! I'm not fucking playing!" she screamed, bucking like a wild horse, hitting my back with the palms of her hands as we entered the building.

I carried her wailing body through the halls until locating the office in question. Knocking quickly, I let myself in and just as I suspected, Judge Dennis was hanging up his robe, about to leave for the weekend.

"Braxton? What a surprise!" he said, eyeing Alexandria curiously. "What brings you by?"

Judge Richard Dennis was a close family friend, one I had known for years and had been instrumental in my career advancement. He wrote an outstanding recommendation letter for law school and spoke to Mr. Paul at the Etose Firm about my capabilities. He was a role model and my most trusted mentor.

"Help! He's kidnapped me!"

"Judge, you think you can marry us?" I asked, skipping the pleasantries.

He frowned, taking another look at Alexandria, still violently wiggling over my shoulder.

"Ummm… right now?"

"Yes, right now, if you don't mind?"

He hesitated, glancing at his blonde court clerk, Helen, sitting at her mahogany desk in the corner. She crossed her arms, annoyed by our sudden presence.

"Uhhh… and you think your… uhhh… friend here wants to?"

"NO!" Alexandria screamed.

"Yes, she wants to," I corrected.

"Really," he laughed. "Well, usually you carry your bride over the threshold after the wedding."

"Cold feet. Trust me, she's ready."

He took another glance at Helen before letting out an uneasy chuckle and shrugged.

"Alright. Let me just get my book. Helen, would you pull up the forms please?"

He disappeared into his chambers as the clerk rolled her blue eyes at me. My unexpected visit was keeping her longer than she intended. Her tits looked good as hell, though. Ignoring the hostility, I walked over to the leather sofa near the window and threw Alexandria down like a sack of potatoes.

"Owww!" she screamed, fumbling to get her bearings. She stared up at me with her gorgeous dark eyes, furious.

"Listen, we have to do this now or your insurance is going to double on Monday, and Dr. Keegan isn't exactly the cheapest doctor on the block."

"Oh, so you're forcing me to marry you just so you can save some money? Be damned if you did it for love!"

I grinned. These types of outbursts used to irritate me to the point of insanity. But now they're entertaining. In fact, comical, seeing her fist clenched up, cheeks puffed, and eyes wild like a ferocious puppy.

"Look, let's just do this now so we have the proper paperwork and we'll worry about the big production shenanigans later. Alright?"

And exactly how I presumed, her eyes eased up. She liked that idea, but would never concede to that fact.

"Fine," she barked. "But I don't like you. Not one bit!"

"That's fine," I said with a nonchalant shrug, just as Judge Dennis stepped out of his office.

"Ok, let's… uh… get started. Helen, would you stand as a witness?"

I yoked Alexandria up to her feet and she stood with her arms crossed. Judge Dennis ran through the procedure as she continued to sulk, sucking her teeth at every other word. She glanced at her watch, tapping her foot on the carpet, as if we were holding her up from nothing. I wanted to shake the shit out of her.

"Do you, Braxton Earwood, take Alexandria Stone to be your lawfully wedded wife?"

"I do," I said, staring down at her scrunched up face as she rolled her eyes in response.

"And do you," Judge Dennis started cautiously, "Alexandria Stone, take Braxton Earwood to be your lawfully wedded husband?"

The entire room paused in suspense. Alexandria gazed around, rocking on her heels, humming. Fucking humming!

Like a damn child, I swear!

"Alexandria," I growled.

She sucked her teeth and checked her nails. Judge Dennis threw me a nervous glance.

"Alexandria!"

"Aight! Yeah, yeah, yeah, whateva. I do," she snapped in her thick New York accent.

Judge Dennis raised an eyebrow but continued, "Then by the power vested in me by the State of Georgia, I now pronounce you husband and wife. You may now… uh… kiss your bride."

"Gah," she snorted and I grinned, only because I accomplished the last item on my things to do list for the day.

#10 Marry Alexandria.

I stepped towards her, cupping her pouty face. Her once stormy eyes softened in my gaze. There was something about her eyes that made it hard to focus at times. They held a thousand emotions, none of which she was able to hide very well, although she tried. But, my dick gets hard every time

I look into them. She gulped and stared up at me, right before I tongued her down, clutching her closer to me, erasing all of her pent up tension.

She's too easy.

With a nip of her bottom lip, I let go and steadied her before she lost her balance. Her eyes lit up, face shocked. She knows I hate public displays of affection, but it was necessary for the moment. She mouthed a 'whoa,' eyes crossing slightly.

After we signed the necessary paperwork and paid the fee, Helen made copies of our license and walked it down to the state office for filing. Alexandria stood by the door, quiet and somber, probably daydreaming, as she often did. She had a tendency to get lost in her own world.

"Thanks Judge. Forgive me for the last minute request. I owe you one," I said, shaking his hand. Alexandria snarled and walked out.

"It's quite alright, Braxton," he said, still a little bewildered over the last thirty minutes spent in his office. "Let's schedule lunch sometime next month."

"Sure. Will do, sir," I said and followed a sullen Alexandria out of the courthouse.

A few orange streetlights illuminated the empty parking lot, the sun out of sight. As we strolled back to the car, I reviewed our marriage license for the third time, just to ensure she signed it properly, using her real name and not a fake one. She was that childish. I planned to fax it to my insurance company as soon as we reached home.

Alexandria was still pretty quiet. She stared at the ground with slumped, defeated shoulders.

"Well, that was easy," I said cheerfully, knowing my demeanor would drive her insane.

"I hate you," she mumbled, stomping her feet.

"Yeah, I know, and that's fine, MRS. Earwood!" Her head shot up at the sound of her new name.

"Yuck," she seethed and bolted ahead of me. And at that very moment, something about the way her ass moved in her jeans, how her shoulders arched back, and the sight of the back of her long neck, made me want her. Bad.

Just as we reached the car, I skipped ahead of her to open the door. The back door.

"What is this? Now you're driving Ms. Daisy?"

I smiled. "Just get in."

Confused, she hesitated for a moment before climbing into the truck. I followed, pushing her along the cream leather seats before closing the door behind me.

"What are you doing?" she snapped but I was focused on her lips. Thick, pouty pink, and tasty. I gripped her waist and pulled her towards me. Her body froze at my touch as I kissed the spot on her neck right below her ear.

"What are you doing?" she repeated, her voice softening as she weakly tried to squirm away.

"It's our honeymoon," I replied, muffled as I kissed the back of her neck. She smelled like oranges and baby powder. Her body started to melt. I was tackling her defenses.

"Really? In the back of the car? Gee, how romantic." She chuckled as if she thought I was joking, but I wasn't. I pulled her on top of me, eased up her shirt, and slid a hand around her breast. She squirmed but I locked my other hand around the back of her neck, holding her still. She let out a small moan.

Not talking shit now, huh?

A quickie was all I needed.

I laid her down across the seat and ripped off her jeans as she pulled at mine, pushing them down to my ankles. I slammed on top of her and she didn't fight me. She opened up and I slid in quick, leveling myself with the door and back of the seat.

"Ohhh... Braxton... but we're in the... ohhhh... I–"

"Shut up."

I flipped her on her stomach and she pushed against the window. I slammed into her, grabbing a handful of her thick ass. My strokes were banging her into the car door. I liked her in this position.

Damn, she feels so good.

"Braxton... AH... Braxton," she screamed as the truck rocked.

Her hair unraveled, draping over her shoulder. I grabbed hold of her long ponytail and pulled back, whispering in her ear.

"You don't like it? Your new name?"

"No... no... I love it," she moaned as I bite her earlobe. The glass began to fog. I grabbed Alexandria's shoulders and her back arched, skin hot under my touch. Her pussy started to throb around me and I rammed into her harder.

"You sure?"

"Yes… yes, I… oh, oh, oh… ah!"

"You gonna cum?"

She let out a pent-up scream and deflated.

"Yeah, that's what I thought."

Shit this feels good.

My nut threatened to explode and I yanked her hair, just for being such a ridiculous fucking person this afternoon, before finishing with a groan.

Good thing I put those tints on last week.

We collapsed and laid curled up in the back seat. All I kept thinking was that I was out of shape and needed to hit a gym. Shouldn't have taken that much out of me to make her cum. Alexandria snuggled up to my chest, dozed and sated. She always conked out after sex. I watched her chest rise and fall, shooting short puffs of air through her nose. She could be hard, stubborn, and downright bitchy sometimes, but she was so peaceful and beautiful when she slept.

I'll give her another five minutes.

It wasn't my first choice to marry Alexandria. I always presumed I would get married someday, just never thought it would be to her. From the moment we met, five years ago, we've had more ups and downs than the average rap music career. But our relationship has been far from average. People used to ask if I regretted fucking her. After all, she was only a jump off, barely had a friends-with-benefits status. To say I used her is a bit strong, but not a complete lie. However, I wasn't ready for fatherhood, nor the responsibilities that came along with it. Regardless, I don't believe in regret and I wasn't about to turn out like my Pops.

We still had forty-five minutes on the sitter clock but the kids were probably antsy. The length of their patience matched their mother's. My phone vibrated in the driver's seat. I glanced at Alexandria, hoping it wouldn't wake her.

It's probably Tiffany. I'll call her back later when Alexandria is asleep. Hope the word won't spread too quickly that I'm no longer a free man.

Alexandria stirred, her child-like eyes opening. There were moments, days, even weeks where I was completely indifferent about her. Her beauty captivated my attention from the very beginning, and before long, I found myself feigning to be inside her. She had me pussy-whipped like some punk, and a man of my caliber should not be so easily taken. But she was like a fruit fly, buzzing in my face, badgering me with her overemotional nonsense relentlessly. Okay, maybe I was a bit unreasonable. I don't deny that I treated her like shit, or that it was selfish to keep her dangling by a mere string of hope, but what she wanted was more than I was ready to give. And what she was willing to take away, I wasn't ready to let go of.

"Hi," she whispered, gleaming. "How long have I've been out?"

"Couple of minutes."

She stretched with a yawn and scratched the tip of her nose like a baby. I resisted the urge to cuddle her to my chest and stay in the back seat of our car for a bit longer.

She's absolutely adorable.

"Is it time to go?" She cocked her head to the side and frowned. Seconds passed by before I realized I was staring and shook out of my daydream to focus.

"Yeah, just about," I replied and sat up in the backseat, passing her the clothes I had torn off before pulling up my pants.

She sighed with a shrug while dressing. "Oh well, I guess back to the real world."

"Yeah, I guess, MRS. Earwood."

"Quit it! That's not my name," she balked, hooking her bra back together. I snickered and buckled my belt.

It's going to be fun teasing her about this.

I opened the door and stepped out to stretch my legs.

"HEY!" She screamed, covering her half naked body with her shirt. "I'm still getting dressed back here! What's wrong with you?"

I glanced around the empty parking lot. "There's no one else here but us."

"Still, you never know."

"Oh, I'm sure the paparazzi got some great footage of the car rocking," I teased and walked around to the driver's side door. She sucked her teeth and finished dressing, sliding out of the back seat, stumbling over her own feet. I laughed and she cut me a stare.

"I hate you," she mumbled, opening the passenger side door.

I shrugged and climbed into the car. "That's fine. I love *you*," I said, and proceeded to check my Blackberry for any missed messages. Just as I suspected—Tiffany had called and sent a text.

Hey Baby, What R U up 2?

I smiled, remembering the last time I saw her, wearing that blue halter dress showing every curve around her tiny waist.

The way she looked in that dress… that ass… those legs… damn.

I shook away the thought and turned the ignition. Just as I was about to pull off, I noticed the door ajar light and turned to Alexandria. She stood outside the car, eyes bulging, mouth gaped open.

"What the fuck's wrong with you? Get in the car, we have to go!"

Her head snapped as if she had just woken up, then she scrambled into the car. Alexandria fumbled with the door, struggling with the seat belt like she had never used it before.

Shit, I really hope the kids don't inherit her goofiness.

She stopped fidgeting and dug her nails into the sides of her seat, breathing heavy as she stared out the windshield. Something had spooked her stupid.

"You okay?"

"Yeah, I'm fine," she croaked out. "I just… well… I… love you too."

Her face immediately turned red as her eyes locked on the floor.

"Oh," I said, catching wind of her feelings. Right. We had never uttered those words to each other before. It surprised us both that I would be so spontaneous, since I wasn't the type to speak without calculating my every word.

But… do I really love her?

We sat in silence, both contemplating the significance of the historic moment. Real talk, Alexandria was never the quintessential Mrs. Right. She was irritatingly annoying, impatient, and had the air of a spoiled brat with an adult's fuming temper. Yet, I couldn't picture my life without her. Looking past all her faults, bottom line was: she's an incredible mother to our children, something I valued highly. She was bright and witty, whether I'm laughing at her or with her, and, though I can't confirm the exact number of woman I've been with (I stopped counting after fifty), I was sure no other woman felt as good as her.

So maybe I do love her… in a sort of perverse way.

I never doubted she loved me, but I had to admit, it was a relief to actually hear her vocalize it. I cleared my throat to break up the awkward silence.

"Come on, let's go see what your rug rats are up to," I said with a grin, putting the car in drive. She bit her lower lip and nodded, smiling like she was about to explode with happiness. And as crazy as it sounds, I couldn't help but feel the same way.

CHAPTER 2

"Look, Mommy's home!" Mia, our nanny, cheered from the living room as we walked through the door. The first to greet us, however, was Sasha. Our slobbering pit bull ran full speed from the kitchen carrying one of girls' dolls, all chewed up. The kids, sitting on the carpet playing with theirs toys, all looked up with simultaneous gummy grins.

"Sweeties!" Alexandria shrieked, sprinting straight towards them with the same grin. She dove straight into their little circle on the floor as I sat our grocery bags down, watching their reunion from the foyer. No longer tiny, little peanuts; the babies were a crawling, rowdy bunch, eating solid foods and speaking gibberish. It was hard to fathom it had been almost a year since they were born. Today also marked the end of my work sabbatical.

After the first few months, I began to understand what Alexandria was going through while stuck at home, pregnant and immobile. Shit, even I wanted to blow my brain outs just to escape the cabin fever. When your career is your life's focal point, it's almost impossible to detach from the grind. But I loved every minute of it, even if taking care of four infants was no vacation.

"Hi babies, hi guys," Alexandria giggled, scooping up Lil Alexander and Brandi. "I've missed you!"

Bethany and Aiden crawled over to join the pile up. Each one of them shrieked happy baby gibberish, welcoming their mother home. Alexandria smothered them each with kisses.

Once, some grad school chick I was fucking back in D.C. tried to psychoanalyze me, saying the absence of my father and the way I grew up made me cold, reserved, and ruthless. That could very well be true. But one look at my four beautiful children warms me right up. They are the most perfect babies ever. And I'm not saying that because I'm their father, I'm saying it because it's the truth. Never did I imagine the type of love I'd have for them—from the moment they were born. I could never deny them, even with the miraculous circumstances surrounding them. It was inconceivable… wait no, more like fucking impossible, to believe someone could become pregnant while on birth control, and with quadruplets at that. Yet, here they are and time seemed to fly when I was with them. Between the simultaneous diaper rashes, colds, fevers, and colic, Alexandria and I overcame every challenge. The challenges my Pops never appreciated. Admittedly, they're a handful but they're mine.

Each had my lips and complexion (Alexandria calls it walnut, but that sounds fucking stupid to me) and had their mother's almond eyes, perfect nose, and thick ebony hair. As crazy as our relationship was, we managed to make some pretty beautiful babies.

Bethany looked up, noticing me by the door and shrieked. She stretched out, crawling my way. Just like her mother, Beth was fast and impatient. She'll be the first of them to walk for sure. I met her half way and scooped her up in my arms, then Aiden, who'd followed after his sister. They were much heavier than when they were first born, which made them easier to hold and play with without the daunting risk of dropping them.

"Hey, Bethy baby!" I responded. Aiden joined her, babbling as if they were trying to tell me a story.

"Oh, really? Well that's very interesting," I said laughing and joined Alexandria on the floor, completing our little family reunion. They were a crazy little bunch, insistent upon telling us some story we couldn't understand, speaking in their own made-up language.

Mia, admiring from afar, laughed as she tied her long black hair back.

"They're always so happy to see you two," she said, cleaning the toys that were scattered around the living room. I tried to avoid looking down her v-neck at her perky D-cups.

Alexandria stood up, holding Lil Alex and Brandi, while Sasha climbed up her legs, eager to be in her arms too. "Thanks, Mia, how'd everything go?"

"Great! We tried to have snack time but they wanted to play, and I didn't have the extra arms to wrangle them into their PJ's."

"Did Alex have his medication?" Alexandria asked, suddenly serious. She was always overly concerned about Lil' Alex. After doctors told us he was stillborn, and his life saving emergency surgery left us both on edge, we lived each day always waiting for the other shoe to drop, sleeping with one eye open.

"Yup, he sure did. I mixed it in with his sweet potatoes."

Alexandria approved then turned to me. "Well, they're all riled up. No way we'll get them to bed just yet. Should we watch a movie?"

Aiden patted my face, grinning while Bethany pulled and played with my collar, determined to have all of my attention.

"Yeah I think that's wise. We'll just change them down here while they're distracted."

"I'll go get the PJ's before heading out," Mia said and skipped towards the stairs. I sat the kids back on the floor gently as Sasha bombarded past me to sniff their diapers.

"Uh-oh, someone made a poo-poo," Alexandria said. I hated the way she baby-talked them. "Can you bring down some new diapers?"

"Sure," I replied and ran up to the nursery, aka Ground Zero.

Mia's back was facing me as she dug in the dresser.

"Finding another way to get us alone I see," Mia cooed under her breath before turning around. She arched a curious eyebrow at me with a smile. She had a pretty curvy frame for an Indian chick. Perfect olive skin, nice ass, thick lips, and a sexy ass gold nose ring.

"Not today, but maybe some other time," I grinned, knowing I was dangling a carrot I had no interest in giving her.

I fucked Mia a week before Alexandria moved down to Atlanta. She was alright, average at best, but nothing to brag about. I suppose in the back of my mind I was hoping she would've done some type of Kama Sutra move on me, but instead she was loud, talkative, and couldn't take a dick. She had just graduated from nursing school and worked at Atlanta Medical Center part-time. I saw her in the hallway the day the kids were born and asked if she'd be interested in being a part-time nanny. We hired her a couple of weeks ago to prepare for my return back to the office. I was confident in her capabilities, and more at ease knowing it wasn't a complete stranger taking care of my children. Alexandria had no clue about our past and I planned to keep it that way.

"Ha. Whatever you say, Mr. Earwood," Mia cooed, and I grabbed a stack of diapers before heading back downstairs to avoid temptation.

When Mia left, we dressed the kids for bed and turned on a "Baby Genius" DVD. I was determined to have these kids reading by two, but they shared their mother's passion for television. Alexandria and I bookended them on the couch; the kids engrossed in the dancing elephants. Half way through, their little minds couldn't handle the excitement and they fell asleep. We scooped up all four babies and laid them in their cribs.

"Where are you going?" Alexandria asked as I headed back downstairs.

"Just want to check some emails."

She cocked her head to the side with a yawn. "Are you nervous about Monday?"

"No. Just trying to be ahead of the curve." That was lie. Not that I was nervous about rejoining the work force. I had no doubt in my capabilities to pick up where I had left off, and I had positioned myself as an irreplaceable asset to the company. However, business hadn't been great since I left, and everyone's job was in jeopardy. Sharlene, my assistant, forwarded me copies of all the business deals in flux while I was on my extended paternity leave.

"Well, I'm sure Mr. Paul will be very happy to have you back," Alexandria said. "I'm gonna go to bed. Don't stay up too late. Okay?"

I nodded, resisting the urge to kiss her as she gave me an exhausted smile, sluggishly walking to our bedroom. There were days when Alexandria plucked my last nerve, but then there were days when she couldn't be sweeter. Those were the days I almost felt guilty about the chicks still texting me at night.

I made my way to the home office, noticing that it was dust free and smelled like Pine-Sol. Alexandria insisted on keeping it spotless, hoping I'd work from home for good, but that wasn't even an option. I opened my laptop and scanned my email. Sharlene sent minutes from the last departmental meeting, mentioning the hiring of an additional lawyer. Another me. I made a mental note to mention it casually in my morning meeting with Mr. Paul.

The last email was from my cousin Kevin in Washington D.C. He was the co-founder of our real estate company, Earwood Properties, and managed our investments in D.C., Maryland, and Virginia, while I handled North Carolina and Georgia. Ma helped by managing our properties in Boston. The market hadn't been as exceptional as we had hoped. We've had to sell some of our properties just to break even, and I've had to dip into our saving just to make mortgage payments. It was one of the reasons I needed to marry Alexandria. I couldn't afford her medicals bills out of pocket with my business suffering.

Kevin had been insisting I come to D.C. to handle some business. But it was impossible for me to leave Alexandria alone with the kids. It took the two of us to manage the smallest problems, especially with Alexandria being so fucking hard-headed.

My Blackberry vibrated on the table.

R u busy?

Tiffany. I hadn't had a chance to hit her back, and wanted to talk to her. But I also wanted to slip into bed and get head from Alexandria.

Wonder if I could convince her some day of a threesome?

I laughed at the thought of how that conversation would go and texted Tiffany back.

About 2 go 2 bed. TTYL?

U better :-)

I shut my lap top and trucked up the stairs. Right before heading to bed, I check on the kids one last time. Sasha laid sleep on the floor in front of the cribs, their four-legged protector. I, their two-legged protector, wanted to stay locked in front of their cribs as well. Damn, where did the time go, and why did it have to go so fast? Real talk, a part of me couldn't wait to suit up and return to the office, but the other part didn't want to step out the front door. It was my responsibility to take care of them, to make sure they want for nothing, keep a roof over their heads, food in their bellies, and that meant some sacrifices. It was hard to imagine leaving them, even for a few hours.

But at least they'll know I'll always come home.

Alexandria snored as if she hadn't slept in a week, dressed in one of those old stretched out nightgowns she wore when she was pregnant. My dick was too hard for me to even think about closing my eyes. But waking her would mean to risk hearing her whine about sleep.

Fuck it. Sleep when we're dead.

I flipped her over to her back and slipped her panties down to her ankles. Startled by the quick movements, she gasped, her eyes flying open before sucking her teeth.

"What the… shit, Braxton? Ugh… what are you doing?"

"Shhhh… quiet," I said, yanking down my boxers. "Just relax."

"I was relaxed," she snapped and it was just the right amount of smartass mouth that I liked to hear. I love a challenge.

"You really want to sleep right now?" I asked, kissing her from collarbone up to her ears while rubbing a thumb against her pussy. She began to thaw as I nibbled on her ear and kissed around her neck to the other ear. Trembling, her hands glided up my arms to my neck. My thumb was just warming her up when I stuck a finger inside. Juicy and wet; she never disappoints. She let out a small moan and titled her head up. She wanted a kiss, but I wouldn't give in just yet. The key was to drive her crazy so she'd beg for it. And believe me, she always begged for it.

Chapter 3

Five a.m., gym, my favorite time of day.

It's the only time I could manage to break away from both the kids and Alexandria. Four days a week, I do about twenty minutes of cardio before hitting the weights and some core-building exercises I learned from my trainer. It helps with the stress, keeps me focused and healthy.

But that's not the only reason…

She always comes in around five-thirty in extra tight sports bras and short shorts; tall, abs perfect, long black hair in one of those high ponytails, ass un-fucking-believable, a Kim Kardashian look-alike.

She pretends she doesn't notice every dude staring at her as she walks straight to the Stairmaster and begins. First slow, then speeds up, breast bouncing, booty jiggling like Jell-O.

Shit…

It was something nice to look at while I went through my reps: three reps of squats, thirty-pound free-weights. I count them out while watching her booty work in the mirror. By the time I'm done with squats, she is done with her cardio, dries the sweat off her face and chest with a towel, and heads over to the weights near me. We always acknowledge each other, since there were never many of us in the gym that early on a consistent basis. A simple head nod, but nothing more. She handles her business, I continue with mine, while the others ogle over her. They'd lick the sweat off her neck if she allowed them. But me, I'm focused. Bench press, no spotter needed. Her eyes always drifted over to me while she handled her free weights. Always admiring, staring from afar.

Then, when I wrap up and am in my cool down, she wraps as well. I chug some water and head to the locker room. She follows, wiping sweat off her titties. We stop outside our perspective locker rooms and stare at each other. She smirks, takes a step back into the doorway and strips, freeing her huge tits and perfect nipples. I smile in appreciation and take out my dick. She grins wider. We stand there, her playing with her nipple, me, stroking my dick. I picture the type of lunges I could do with her straddled over my shoulder, pussy in my face. Thirty seconds more before I put my junk away and head for the showers. She does the same.

I wash up quick, head to the car, and make it home just as Alexandria and the kids are waking.

It's a fucking awesome way to start the day.

***

I wonder if anyone else's wife packs their lunch the way Alexandria does mine.

I walked off the elevator at The Etose Firm in a crisp new suit, with my leather briefcase and a bright orange lunch bag that was by no means professional. Shit was fucking heavier than my laptop. Alexandria insisted that I take it and I'd rather hear nails on a chalkboard than her complaining if I didn't. A new, much older, receptionist, Ms. Grace, greeted me at the front entrance. The firm's previous one, Victoria, was promoted to Mr. Paul's executive assistant. How she was able to land such a position is questionable, but given our track record, I'm sure her "performance" was enough to seal the deal.

"Good Morning, Mr. Earwood," Sharlene said, greeting me with a cup of coffee and a print-out of my daily schedule. She was at least in her mid-forties, short and slightly pudgy with gigantic breast she didn't bother trying to conceal very well. I always had to divert my eyes when the room got a little chilly. She had a crush on me that I ignored because she was excellent at her job and impossible to replace.

"Morning, Sharlene," I replied, passing her my lunch bag in exchange for coffee. Taking a sip, I walked into my office. It smelled fresh, like it was recently dusted. I took a deep breath, admiring the view of the Atlanta skyline. Felt good to be back.

After the gym, my morning had gone pretty smooth. Alexandria jumped up and made pancakes, cheese eggs, and bacon. I kissed the kids, who were merely confused but not distressed as I walked out the door. Alexandria did her best to hide it, but past the fake smile and jokes about my wardrobe, she seemed despondent. And I knew the culprit of her demeanor: I was on my way to work and her work was at home. She was trying to be a good sport about it by pretending, but I knew her better than she knew herself.

"Just a reminder," Sharlene said from the door. "You have a meeting with Mr. Paul at ten-thirty, then a conference call at twelve, followed by client meeting at one-thirty, an agent meeting at two-thirty and then the departmental is at four. Mr. Paul also wanted you to review Jason Brooks' contracts before the five o'clock conference call, and Dante Jergan's agent called twice this morning; his manager is on line one. And your cousin Kevin is on line two holding for you."

Got damn! It's only 9 a.m. I haven't even put my bag down yet.

The Jason Brooks contract was at least a hundred pages long and was on its tenth revision. It would take at least two hours to review it thoroughly. Two hours I didn't have.

They're not trying to make this easy, huh?

Sharlene clenched her notepad with a worried frown, waiting for a reaction to the insane schedule. I checked myself out in the mirror placed above my sofa and smoothed down my hair, double-checking that my tie was straight and shirt still crisp. Vain, I know, but I didn't give a fuck. Appearance is everything and I refused to allow the office to even think I'd fallen off in any way. I'd always had an assiduous work ethic. Ma said I even took learning my colors serious.

"That's fine," I said tonelessly while booting up my workstation. "Please pull up the Brooks contract, highlight the new appendixes, and tell Kevin to call back at eleven forty five. When I'm off the call with the manager, patch in Dante's agent. Oh, and block off an hour for lunch tomorrow, I need a shape up."

"Yes sir!" Sharlene said, impressed as ever before rushing back to her desk.

#3 Never let them see you sweat.

Couldn't even take a full sip of my coffee before my Blackberry buzzed in my pocket.

"Alexandria, I haven't even been gone a full two hours yet."

"Hey! What's with the gang of Spanish ladies at my door?"

"Oh, good. They're there to clean. Let them in."

"Why?" she scoffed. "You don't like the way I polish the toilet or something?"

Shit, I can't do anything without getting the third degree!

"It's one less chore you have to worry about," I snapped. "Don't you think you have your hands full with the kids?"

"Well… yeah… but…"

"Right. So just load the kids up in the 4X4 and take them for a walk so you can get out of the house for a change."

"Nah, I need to stay here and make sure they don't steal my shoes or something."

"Alexandria! Go!"

"Jeez, ok, ok. And… thanks. This is really thoughtful of you."

I pictured her smiling on the other end of the line and my chest swelled with pride, enough to float back to the house and be wrapped up in her again. Instead, I cleared my throat and regained my composure. "Yup. Right. See you when I get home."

I hung up, sat my coffee down and unpacked my briefcase. Alexandria had planted a couple of framed portraits of the kids in my bag. I placed them on the empty shelves of my bookcase and stepped back to admire them: my children and my reluctant, hardheaded wife. Though I missed them, there was nothing like the smell of new contracts in the morning.

It's good to be back.

***

"Braxton! Welcome back to the real world!"

Mr. Paul greeted me as I walked into his massive office. Victoria showed me in, and also showed she was not over our little misunderstanding last year by giving me the extreme cold shoulder. Her altercation with a very pregnant Alexandria caused some severe embarrassment. Wasn't my fault. She never asked if I had a girlfriend, and even if she did, my response still wouldn't account for the entire truth.

#4 Never give more information than needed.

Alexandria was never my girlfriend. You can say we had an agreement of sorts but never actually made it official. It was insane how we jumped from just fucking to being husband and wife, almost as insane as having quadruplets. If I had told Victoria, the notorious office gossiper, I was expecting, the entire office would have known within a few hours, and I'm not fond of strangers knowing my personal business.

But with a body like that, shiittttt, I'd be a sucker not to hit it.

I didn't though. She sucked my dick a few times, let me palm her ass and suck on her breasts, but I never fucked her and put little effort into pursuing her. It's not in my nature to chase women who come so willing. Like I said, I need a challenge.

"It's great to be back," I said and shook Mr. Paul's hand, throwing Victoria a grin. She rolled her eyes and sashayed out of the office.

"How are the kids? When are you gonna bring them in?" he asked as he took a seat behind his desk. "I've seen them all over the news but I haven't seen them for myself!"

"Excellent, getting bigger every day," I said, taking a seat. "Maybe I'll have Alexandria bring them in next week."

"That'd be great! I can't wait to meet them. Need to get a picture for the wife. She loves them."

Alexandria's sensational pregnancy made every major news headline around the country, not only due to the amount of babies she was expecting, but also due to the surreal circumstances. Without any sort of fertility treatments, she became freakishly pregnant with quadruplets, an anomaly of tremendous proportions. To add another layer to the already peculiar occurrence, Alexandria was on the pill and I damn sure was using condoms. *What the fuck...* that's all I kept asking myself.

To say I had doubts about the possibility of the babies being mine would be an understatement. But there was no fucking way she could have collected my semen without me knowing. Too many successful brothers out there got trapped by women who just "happened" to become pregnant, so I was diligent about disposing condoms myself. So when Alexandria told me, it was a complete mind fuck. I hired the best investigators in the state, ran background checks with various sources, and checked with every known fertility clinic in the country to determine if they could have possibly had her as a patient. Just as Alexandria promised, she had not slept with another man besides me while we were fuck buddies, and never visited a single clinic. Deep down I knew Alexandria was not one to lie. It was one of the qualities I admired about her.

I didn't want kids, not yet. But what's that saying? *Tell God your plan and he laughs at you.* Yeah, he was definitely laughing at my ass. Because from the moment doctors pulled those babies out of her womb, it was like my chest opened up, and I've been breathing different ever since.

Luckily for me, Mr. Paul was a family man and loved children. It was the only way I could have convinced him to let me have almost an entire year off and still keep my position at the firm.

"Braxton, I know you just got back, but we have an emergency," Mr. Paul said, leaning closer.

"I know, Mr. Paul. I talked to Dante's manager this morning," I said, beating him to the punch. Dante Jergan, the star quarterback for the

Washington D.C. Redskins was considering moving to a different agency over stipulations with his contract. Dante was one of our best clients.

"You did? Oh…well, okay then," he said, appearing surprised that I was already on top of things. (*I haven't been gone that long; does he need to be reminded of who he's dealing with?*) "Well, we need to iron this out ASAP. We can't lose him as a client."

"Consider it done, sir."

"But, this isn't something you can handle over the phone," he continued wearily. "You'll have to go to D.C. and meet with them personally."

D.C.? Now? The fuck?

"Sir, with all due respect," I chuckled as if the news was no big deal. "I think it's possible to handle the situation without wasting the travel expense."

"It's not just that. We have a new potential client. Clint Park's assistant called. He's looking for representation. I told her I'd send my best lawyer."

I ran through the few facts I knew about Clint: He was the star pitcher for the Washington D.C. Nationals; one of the highest-paid baseball players in the league; from Los Angeles; playing since he was four. Until recently, he was being represented by a local D.C. firm, but after several issues with his contract and an endorsement deal gone wrong, he fired his agent and lawyer, and was now a piece of fresh meat walking out in the desert, surrounded by vultures.

"Sir, I'm never one to object, but this is a bit untimely, given my domestic circumstances. Not that the children are burdensome or that Alexandria is incapable, but I doubt I'll be able to leave."

#7 Speak intelligently. It throws victims off.

Mr. Paul only nodded then shrugged as if to say "your loss," and I held an unaffected disposition. Just short of two hours back on the job and my boss was already looking at me different.

"Braxton, I understand about family responsibilities, believe me. But you're one of our best attorneys and you have a bright future ahead of you here. Some commitments… might need to take a back seat for the sake of your growth, which would subsequently help your family in the long run."

Mr. Paul couldn't possible have understood. Which was probably why his wife cheated on him regularly, according to office gossip. He was never home enough to notice. I'd kill Alexandria if she ever pulled some shit like that on me.

My Blackberry buzzed in my pocket, interrupting us. Mr. Paul jumped like it was his phone.

"You better get that, it might be Alex!"

Alexandria wouldn't dare to call me so soon. I pulled out my phone as Mr. Paul watched, creeping to the edge of his seat as if the end was near.

Shit man, pull yourself together.

Morning sunshine! Sleep well? BTW When are you coming to D.C.?

Tiffany. Her usual morning text message, a sign I was her first thought in the morning. It always made me smile, even at the most inopportune times. How ironic she mentioned D.C. in the middle of meeting about potential travel there.

Perhaps it's a fortuitous sign.

I looked up, realizing Mr. Paul was staring at me.

"Sorry, it was my cousin," I lied, then changed gears. "Perhaps you're right. A little face-to-face time with a potential client might be beneficial. I'll talk to Alexandria, I'm sure I can make arrangements."

***

Ma always said I was a quiet and perceptive child from the day I was born. "Barely cried in the delivery room, just came out, eyes open, soaking up his new world."

I was her first son and third after my two older sisters, Melissa and Nina. My Pops wasn't there for the delivery, hardly there throughout their entire marriage. Everyone in the neighborhood knew he was a rolling stone, but my Ma thought she could change him over time. Got a wakeup call when just two weeks after I was born, my Pops came in the door with another newborn, another son, my brother Brian. Even though I'm sure it hurt, Ma couldn't turn the child away.

We were raised together like twins. Brian's real mother lived just down the block, but didn't have time for a baby between her partying and crack pipe. As we grew older, the differences between us were evident. I was naturally intelligent and highly observant; school was effortless. I was reading at a second grade level before I started kindergarten. Brian, on the other hand, was struggling to keep up with basic reading and mathematics up until middle school. During a spelling bee in fourth grade, I spelled a particularly difficult word, never having seen or heard it before. Soon after, I was placed in an advance learning program and skipped a grade. He called me a corny ass nerd.

That's what I always think of when I watch Aiden and Lil Alex play together, wondering which one of them will be me and which one will be Brian, and how I can stop history from repeating itself.

"Your mother wants to have the kids christened."

Alexandria's voice zaps me back as she sets a plate of spaghetti and meat sauce in front of me.

"Ok.... so?"

"Means we can have a party," Alexandria grinned, while fixing herself a plate. We were eating in the dining room while the kids played bumper cars in their walkers around us.

"Oh lord," I grumbled.

"What?"

"It means you're going to go into insane planning mode."

I imagined her creating a new O.C.D.-like schedule board, surpassing the one she already made for the kids daily.

"Braxton! Don't be so selfish," she said with a smirk. "It's for our children, to save their souls!"

"Yeah, I'm sure."

"Pleasssse! It'll be so much fun. Our whole family could come. It'll be like a big house party. What do you think?"

I twirled my fork around my plate. "I think parties are expensive."

She sulked as Aiden bumped into my chair again. He stared up at me, tickled by something, before shrieking all sorts of baby babble. That's the best part about having babies—no matter what, they're always excited to see you.

It wasn't until I turned eight that my Pops left for good. He had just dropped off another newborn, my sister Megan, while my mother was five months pregnant with my baby sister Paris. We didn't really notice the difference from his absence since he wasn't around much anyways. What we did miss was the little money my father contributed. We were stretching every dime of government assistance just to feed one another. There were days my mother didn't eat, just to save enough for us. Surviving the Boston winters with little to no heat... I wouldn't wish that on nobody.

"How have you been holding up, on your own that is?" I asked, distracting myself from any further thoughts about a man who was practically dead to me. We only hired Mia for three days a week. The other days, Alexandria was manning the house solo.

She shrugged. "It's going ok. It's exhausting even with help, but I'm managing. It'll be a mad house once these kids learn how to walk."

Brandi bumped into my chair and giggled, starring up at me with her mother's eyes. I smiled back, gently pushing her walker back with my foot. Alexandria cut up some manageable pieces of pasta and slid them on a plate for Lil Alex. They giggled at each other. I loved seeing her this way, an adorable mother. Which made having our next conversation that much more dreadful, knowing she was about to turn back into the nagging tantrum-throwing tyrant I knew well.

Might as well get this over with.

"I have to go to D.C. next week."

Alexandria did a Looney Tunes double take. "Say what?"

I sighed and avoided her glare. "For work. Mr. Paul wants me to meet with a new client."

"No."

"Alexandria…"

"No! You're not leaving me here by myself!"

She jumped up, grabbing the empty breadbasket and plates.

"You've only been back to work one day and they already got you traveling? No!"

I followed her to the kitchen, keeping my voice low and toneless, only because I knew it drove her crazy. The kids bumped into each other trying to follow us.

"I can see if Mia is available to come for an extra few days," I offered.

"I don't want Mia! I want you!"

She dumped our empty dishes and pots into the sink, violently attacking them with her sponge. She could be such a fucking child.

"Alexandria, I have to go. Plus, there's a couple of other things I have to do there, too."

"Really? Like what?" she snapped.

Tiffany was my first thought but I was sure Alexandria didn't want to hear that. She dropped her dish towel on the floor and scooped it up. It was a simple act, but it was all I needed to see, her thick ass drop low in her thin grey leggings. I stepped behind her, smoothing my hand up her thigh and cupping what was mine. She flinched but didn't push me away. I wrapped my arms around her waist, pushing my dick against her ass.

"Trying to sell a property," I whispered in her ear. "We need the money. You want a ring, don't you?"

She stiffened, biting her lip. She wanted a ring bad enough that even the thought distracted her.

"Fine," she sighed. "You can go, but under one condition."

Like I really need your permission.

She pushed and wiggled her ass back on me. At that moment I would've given her anything she wanted.

"What's that?"

I eased my hand up her shirt, pinching her nipple. She wasn't wearing a bra, which was hot as fuck. I'd been staring at her tits all through dinner.

"And you can't take it back," she moaned, leaning her head back against my chest. I pressed a finger against her crotch, pushing her harder against my dick.

"What do you want, Alexandria?" The question was two-fold.

"You have to let me have the party," she exhaled and I slipped a finger inside her, warm and wet as ever. She let out another moan, right before a walker hit the back of my leg. I looked down at Bethany staring up at me with a grin. Kind of forgot the kids were still in the room and immediately lost my hard-on.

I wasn't completely opposed to the idea. But the type of production Alexandria would want—having an elaborate party for the kids that they would never remember—was pointless and unnecessary. However, my family visiting wasn't such a bad idea, and it would make my Ma happy.

"Fine," I relented. "Now, can we put these kids to bed so I can get *you* into bed?"

***

"Okay, Alex, over here… Brandi—Brandi sweet girl over here, look… Aiden, look over here!"

The photographer stood behind his mounted camera and shook a rattle at the kids, who were starring back wide-eyed in fright. He was pretty scary looking with his tight black leather pants, slicked back graying ponytail, pointed eyebrows, and his nose, chin, and eyebrow piercing.

Alexandria and I stood on the sidelines at the cover shoot for *Parents* magazine, watching the baby handlers, assistants, and editors fussing over our children. The kids were dressed in matching sage green jumpers, sitting on the floor in front of a white backdrop, blinding lights surrounding them; their faces puzzled and strained.

"This is ridiculous," I mumbled, my arms tightening.

When the editors at *Parents* approached us, the deal they presented was impossible to turn down: an exclusive yearly cover story, paying ten grand per year. Five years' worth of covers would pay at least two years of college for at least one of the kids.

Middle America was obsessed with our miracle bunch. We had turned into mini-celebrities, featured in *People, Time, US Weekly, Essence* and countless newspapers. We tried to take it in stride. But just walking down the street had become a challenge when photographers would pop out of bushes. Alexandria and I shielded the kids as much as we could until the sensation died down. But I didn't expect such a circus at a photo shoot.

Alexandria stood by my side, shifting and blowing out air every two minutes.

"Why the hell do they have a makeup artist here?" she asked. "They're eleven months. And why does that woman have a curling iron?"

Bethany patted at the white ribbon in her hair, perplexed, as Aiden pulled on Lil Alex's shirt.

Donald Murphy, editor-in-chief of the magazine, approached us. "Hi, guys!"

The five foot three hot shot New Yorker air kissed Alexandria in his ultra-sheen blazer, skinny jeans and heeled boots that helped add an inch to his dwarf like height.

"Hey… Donald," Alexandria said, stepping closer to me. His proximity made her uncomfortable. Alexandria hated strangers.

"The kids look great," he said. "They're growing up so fast."

"I know," she said, with a tinge of disappointment. I wanted to rub her shoulders but stopped myself. I don't know why.

"Ummm… Donald," I started, watching one of the assistants brush Brandi's hair. Brandi scowled, swatting her away. "Is all of this really necessary?"

Donald turned as if noticing the shoot for the first time, oblivious to the pretentious scene surrounding the kids. He probably has never touched a baby in his life, let alone had a shred of an idea what being a parent entailed. Just as he tried to convince us everything was fine and that all cover shoots were like this, the photographer, frustrated by his uncooperative models, threw the rattle on the ground with a groan. Startled, Brandi's lips quivered before she burst into tears.

"Damn," Alexandria grumbled and rushed towards her, but a red-headed assistant jumped in her path, arms extended.

"Whoa, whoa, wait a second. You can't go on the set!"

Alexandria did a double take. "Excuse me?"

Uh-oh.

Sensing her temper rising, I rushed past Donald and grabbed Alexandria's arms, holding her back.

"Calm down. Let me handle this," I whispered in her ear. She nodded, her stony eyes locking on the unfortunate assistant like a lioness, fiercely protective over her cubs. Brandi was wailing, searching frantically for Alexandria.

"Hi. We just want to check on the kids. They've never participated in something like this and we want to ensure they're ok."

"They're ok," she nodded, as if she was deaf to Brandi's cries. "We can take care of them. That's what we're here for. You two might just distract them."

Alexandria bucked at her again and I roped my arms around her waist. I loved it when she got like this, feisty and aggressive; it kind of turned me on.

"My baby is crying," she grumbled at me. "You have five seconds left of this diplomatic shit before I hit her."

The assistant flinched but held her ground.

"Miss, I'm warning you," I chuckled. "Let us through or I'll let her go."

"Let them through, Michelle," Donald said behind us. Michelle frowned, crossing her arms.

"But the set—"

"Just let them through," he sighed. Even he was losing his patience with her.

Michelle huffed before stepping out of the way. Alexandria wiggled out of my arms and rushed through the crowd, picking up Brandi in one scoop.

"Ok, ok. Now what's with all the tears, kid? Mommy's right here!"

Brandi calmed in her mother's arm as Alexandria wiped the tears off her chubby cheeks, showering her with kisses. Lil' Alex crawled over towards her leg, letting out a happy screech. Alexandria sat on the floor, Indian style and let the kids crawl over her, giggling.

They are so in love with their mother.

As much as she swore she wouldn't be, Alexandria was an amazing mother, above and beyond my expectations. Unconventional, of course, but I had worried for nothing. Motherhood came naturally to her.

"Braxton, pass me that toy," Alexandria said while smothering Bethany with kisses.

I grabbed the toy, dusting it off before giving the photographer a sly grin. He only stared as I walked on to the set, sitting on the floor next to them. Aiden and Bethany crawled into my lap, squealing.

"Oh, you wanna fly, tough guy!"

I lifted Aiden over my head, whisking him around like an airplane and he giggled.

For a moment, it was just us playing on the floor like we did at home, and I almost forgot about the crowd of people and cameras surrounding us. Until Donald said, "You know what, shoot it."

"Shoot it?" The photographer questioned, indignant.

"Yeah, leave them in the shot. I want to capture this."

"But we didn't do their hair or makeup," Michelle whined from somewhere. "Or their wardrobe!"

"What are you blind?" Donald asked. "They look beautiful! Just take it."

With a huff, the photographer shrugged and gave a signal to his team.

Donald stepped closer to the set. "You two mind if we include you in the shot?"

I shrugged as Alexandria looked down at her faded light blue jeans and white t-shirt.

"Dag, my first cover shoot and I look a mess."

Her long hair flowed over her shoulders, cheeks with a faint pink blush that matched her lips. She was radiant.

"You look like a mom," I said and pulled her closer, feeling that weird urge again to touch her. "It's a good look on you."

She smiled, blushing and shying away from my stare. "Thanks."

She loved compliments but I didn't give them out often. Didn't want her head getting too big. But I liked her this way the best; sexy, natural, all mine. I wanted to kiss her neck but stopped myself, glancing down at the kids. All eyes fixed on us, smiling.

"Ok," I laughed, scooting closer to her. "We're ready."

CHAPTER 4

"Who is it?" Kennedy's voice snapped from the other side of the condo door.

"It's Bad Habit," I said, chuckling at the crazy nickname Alexandria bestowed upon me. The lock snapped and the door swung open. Kennedy, Alexandria's best friend and my worst nightmare, stood bracing herself, wearing a thin red satin night gown that barley came to her mid-thigh and no bra to support her enormous titties. I diverted my eyes from them and stared into her narrowing ones. Last time I saw her, her hair was cut in a short black bob. Now she had a long brown weave, similar to the basketball and football wives I've seen on TV. Alexandria loved those shows.

"You said you'd be here three hours ago," she snapped.

I shrugged, not feeling the need to give her an explanation of my whereabouts or tardiness. Anything and everything else was more important than her.

She rolled her eyes realizing she wasn't going to get an apology and swung the door wider to let me stroll in. My old one-bedroom apartment, my home throughout law school, located on a quiet block in Southwest, Washington D.C., now had more of a woman's touch to it—with fancy paintings, brightly-colored walls, and soft lighting—from the tight living room, to the narrow hallway where the kitchen was lined, to the small dining area. Opposite the kitchen, was the entrance to my old bedroom; way more girly than I ever had it, with some long silky curtains, a pink comforter, and white dressers. It smelled like she had just lit some vanilla candles. Without waiting for an invitation, I sat on her sky blue couch in the living room by the windows facing her massive flat screen TV. Kennedy sucked her teeth and stomped past the coffee table over to the matching love seat. There was a gold trim mirror hanging on the adjacent wall.

I fucked Alexandria on that very wall.

"So what's up?" she snapped.

"Here, her royal highness sends gifts."

I passed Kennedy a gift bag with framed pictures of her four soon-to-be godchildren. Her face lit up.

"Oh my gosh! They're so adorable," she said, flipping through the pictures. "Thank God they took after their mother."

Oh brother.

"She also said you had something for them," I said, growing more irritated by the second.

Kennedy disappeared into the bedroom and returned with a couple of large shopping bags. "I bought them some new outfits. Now, these are a few sizes too big but they'll grow into them in a month or so. Aren't they cute?"

She grinned, taking the little jumpers, dresses, and hats out, modeling them. Unimpressed, I relaxed my legs and took out my Blackberry to check my email. She must have measured my mood and shoved the clothes back into the bags.

"Here," she said, throwing the bags in my lap. "Take it. You can go now!"

Without even looking at her, I placed the bags on the floor and straighten my shirt, unintentionally brushing off my shoulders.

"Real mature," I chuckled. "I see you haven't changed."

"You can kiss my ass!"

"The same way you can suck my dick. Oh wait, you've already done that."

Her eyes widened, mouth dropping and I smiled. I'm not one to bring up the past, but when the opportunity presents itself, I can't resist.

"You're fucking disgusting," she hissed out.

"That's fine," I replied, unable to stop grinning while I finished up a text.

Kennedy bit her lip, fidgeting with the ends of her nightgown, wheels spinning in her head.

"You haven't... told her anything, have you?" she asked with a wince.

I fucked Kennedy; a couple of months after I met Alexandria and before I broke up with my ex. And hell yeah, I regretted it. I took Kennedy's drunk ass home one night after the club when Alexandria was out of town. Kennedy knew about my relations with her best friend but had little regard for it. One thing led to another and next thing I knew she was climbing on top of my dick. It wasn't even a challenge. She was good, but Alexandria was better, with the type of pussy you could just melt into, which made keeping her a secret from my friends (and my then-girlfriend), that much more... imperative. I don't know why but I wasn't willing to share. I didn't even want people to know Alexandria existed. I wanted to keep her all to myself, a buried treasure.

But Kennedy refused to understand her hit-it-and-quit-it status. She had all the ill qualities of a groupie. I ignored her non-stop calls, texts, and in turn, she became belligerent and obsessive. Once she realized I had no interest, her obsession turned into hatred, subsequently using Alexandria as an unknowing vehicle to express it. When Alexandria came back to town, she confronted me with this ludicrous story that Kennedy had allegedly seen me with some "other" girl.

Alexandria and I always had our issues, but they exasperated after I fucked her friend. I concluded Kennedy was the type of manipulative bitch who liked playing high school games. The thought of her being my children's godmother disgusted me, but I had no choice. Alexandria still had no clue what had happened between us.

"If I told her, you think she would be sending you pictures?" I huffed.

A guilty expression crumbled her face. She shook her head and stood up, her nightgown flowing. She wasn't wearing any panties.

I really wish she'd put some real clothes on.

It amazed me how stupid women could be. They have unwavering trust for each other but have little trust in men, unaware that their best friend is the one they should be more concerned with. Many of the arguments Alexandria and I have had in the past seemed to be in direct relation to Kennedy's coaching. As if she was handing her the script to read. Men could never be as devious and manipulative as women, we're simple creatures.

"Would you like something to drink?" she asked.

"What do you have?"

"Vodka, Hennessey, Bacardi..."

Kennedy meant alcohol but I wasn't there to have a good time. I only did this so Alexandria wouldn't nag me to death.

"I'll take some water."

Her eyebrow arched as she strolled into the kitchen, meticulously pouring the water nightcap as if she was a dramatic bar tender.

"How's the place?" I asked, switching gears.

"It's cool. Right by the red line so it only takes me ten minutes to get to work."

Kennedy's lease was up at her old apartment and I needed a new tenant. Strictly business, trusting her off the strength of Alexandria. At least she paid her rent like clockwork.

"Neighbors give you any trouble?"

"Not lately."

"Toilet?"

"Works fine now, thanks for sending that plumber." She grinned. "How's your wife?"

Alexandria had told her, of course. It'd only been a week.

Wonder how many people Kennedy gossiped that off to?

"She's fine. Busy with the kids. How's your quarterback?"

Her eyes bulged; surprised by my knowledge of the new, married Washington Redskins quarterback she had been fucking.

"Yeah, Alexandria tells me things too," I chuckled. She adjusted her face with a huff.

"Whatever. I just can't believe you guys got married," she said with a sigh, twirling a piece of hair around her finger. "All seems soooo… fast. First, all those babies then marriage. You just never struck me as the family-man type."

My muscles tightened around my neck. "What's that supposed to mean?"

"I don't know, you don't seem like the type of dude who would settle down. More like a rolling stone type."

Like my Pops?

Honestly, I never saw myself as the family man either. Well, at least not so soon. I knew someday I'd get married and have a rack of kids, just not all at once. But did people really see me like that? Did I give off that type of vibe? Maybe it was because I was always practical, pragmatic, and fully researched my options. Even if some of those options were two best friends.

I wonder if Ma saw that in Pops?

Lost in my own thoughts, I chugged down the water, handed her my cup, and rose to my feet.

"It's getting late. I better go."

"It's late and you just got here!"

"I told Alexandria I'd call her around midnight." That was a lie. Alexandria had probably fallen asleep around nine after putting the kids to bed.

"Well… are you gonna come back?" Kennedy squirmed, wrapping her arms around herself, her voice pleading and desperate.

Is she lonely? Is she in need of male company or something?

Not my problem but I figured I'd go easy on her with my most used non-committal answer.

"Maybe."

***

"Well look who it fucking is–Braxton Smooth in the mother-fucking building!"

Rocs dapped me up by the door of Josephine's, one of the hottest clubs in D.C. Nothing but pristine service, athletes, and sexy ass women. I blew past the line wrapped around the block and went through the VIP entrance.

Lines are for commoners and I'm no common dude.

Rocs was a little hood dude from New Jersey I'd known since undergrad that had made a name for himself as a party promoter.

"Yo, I thought you moved down to ATL?" he asked.

"Yeah I did, just came up to handle some business."

"Well, welcome back! You getting a table?"

"Of course man! Don't I always?"

"Aight kid, let me set you up."

We moved through the crowd as a waitress showed us to a table near the stage, handing me the bottle service menu. Club scenes can make you feel like you're inside a shark tank. The moment you walk in and do something out of the norm, every female pays attention. I was scheduled to meet my future client, Clint, at midnight but I didn't expect him to arrive until closer to one. Athletes were never on time for meetings and never arrived to clubs earlier than necessary. It was a part of the territory that I had to readjust to. I ordered two Red Bulls and two bottles of Moet Rose as Rocs joined me.

"Jess, add another bottle to the order. It's a celebration!"

Rocs and I talked business as the club started popping, packed wall to wall with some lovely memories…

"Hey, Smooth." Cindy, a doctor from Texas. Used to throw down a mean soul food dinner every Sunday.

"Hi, Smooth." Patricia, from California, worked in finance. Met her at a charity event. So refined… and fine.

"Haven't seen you in while. Where you been?" Toya, from… well, who cares where she was from or what she did. Her body was banging.

Rocs shook his head and laughed every time I dodged their questions.

"Damn dude, the bitches been missing you," he said, pouring himself another glass of champagne. I agreed with him just as two ladies I didn't recognized slid behind the velvet rope, joining our table.

"Hi, Rocs," they said in unison. The chick with a low cut, backless blouse and tight jeans eased onto Rocs lap. She was at least two feet taller than him with a stick figure and money hungry eyes.

"Hey, ladies," Rocs said. "Say hello to my friend."

Her friend, a more voluptuous type of chick, dressed in a black body suit sat next to me, placing her Gucci tote on the table.

"Hey, what's your name?" she asked, licking her lips. I held back an eye-roll as I told her. "Braxton," she repeated twice, rolling my name off her tongue, eye-fucking me while pouring herself a drink. Her name was Trina, worked in sales. Whatever that meant.

"You're cute. You single?" she asked, flipping her hair back. Her hand smoothed up my thigh as her nails grazed my dick. She was bold. I liked that.

"Not quite." That wasn't a lie. I'm not quite a single man. We made some small talk as her friend continued to help herself to my liquor. Off the bat, I knew these were some basic bitches, but I figured it's the best way to kill time until Clint arrived.

"Hmmm… you got any kids?"

"Yep." I was a proud parent. I wasn't like other dudes who lied about having kids. I made it a point that if someone asked me outright, I'd respond truthfully.

Unlike my father.

"How many you got?"

But here's where it gets sticky..."Four."

"FOUR! Nigga you got four kids? Oh hell to the no!" she screamed, snatching her hand back as if she touched a hotplate.

Her friend looked over at Rocs and laughed.

"Trina, what's wrong?"

"This nigga got four kids!"

"Four? How many baby mommas?"

The whole table stared. I took another sip of my drink. Since I didn't care what neither of these broads thought of me, their questions were simple to answer.

"I have one."

Trina's neck snapped back, the concept unheard of.

"Oh wait," The model said, jumping in Rocs lap. "You're that guy! The one who had all them kids! The… what's it called… quadruplets, right?" She turned to Trina. "Yo, I heard about him. He got some chick on birth control pregnant. He got that super sperm girl!"

The two of them drunkenly cackled, tickled by their own jokes as Rocs raised an eyebrow.

"Yo, is that true man?"

Just as I was about to respond, my new potential client stepped up to our table.

"I see you started the party without me," Clint said with a grin, taking in the scene.

"Clint, pleasure to meet you." I stood, shaking the hood rat off of me and extending a hand. His grip was firm, the true sign of a mighty pitcher. He was tall, almost albino in color, with long jet black hair tied in a curly pony tail, a combination of his Mexican mother and African father.

"Good to meet you too, man," he said with a grin. "Heard a lot about you. This table's kinda small. I got a room in back tho'."

He smirked as the girls exchanged glances, drooling over his diamond encrusted Rolex and rings.

No way I'll be able to seal this deal with these gold diggers around.

I pat Rocs on the back and offered my hand.

"So man, I'mma holla at you later. We got some business to discuss."

Rocs nodded and dapped me up. "No problem man. I'll holla at you later."

I followed Clint through the crowd to a VIP suite in the back where another party had started without him. His entourage was popping bottles on his dime. Girls flocked around them but at least they were of higher quality than Rocs' chickenheads.

A waitress came and took our drink orders. Clint had a reputation on the D.C. party scene, spending more in one night than people made in two weeks. It wasn't the most ideal place to talk business, since I couldn't hear myself think over the thumping music, but I had to start playing hardball. Only had a week to convince him our firm would be his best representative.

"So how you liking D.C.?" I shouted over the music.

He grinned over his shot of Patron. "Don't you mean how am I liking the Nationals?"

At least he's not slow.

We laughed and stared out into the crowded club as the DJ switched to reggae. Not bad for a Wednesday night.

"D.C. is aight, man," Clint said. "They treat me well. I can't complain. Except the money could be better."

Since Clint joined the team, ticket sales had gone up and he was drowning in endorsements opportunities. He was a star rookie, found pitching 80mph on some minor league team. How he was overlooked for so many years, no one knew, but the Nationals got him dirt cheap. His contract needed some serious revamping.

"I think you have some tremendous opportunities available to you. Most importantly, the Nationals aren't going to want to lose you, so you have some bargaining points. I'm willing to go to bat for you, no pun intended."

Clint choked out a laugh as we cheers another round of Patron shots followed by limes. A chick eyeing us from the corner of the VIP licked her glossy wet lips at me.

Hmmm.

"Imma be honest with you man," Clint said and I refocused. "I was kinda shocked to see you. I was expecting some young Jew-looking dude. I need to know the folks working for me got my back and that they my peoples. Not some stuck up uppity, you smell me?"

So that's why he set this meeting up in a club? This is a test.

And I was ready to pass without a doubt.

"So you've been burned before, I take it?"

"Nah, I just don't trust white folks!"

We laughed as the waitress refilled our glasses while the model from the corner positioned herself next to me. She poured herself a shot and sucked the shit out of her lime, never losing eye contact.

The girl's got talent. She could be interesting.

Clint and I joked and laughed for the rest of the night. He was pretty cool and had a good head on his shoulders, which wasn't average for athletes. I could even envision us chilling outside of work. But I hadn't secured him as a client yet, and that came first. Just as I was about to dive into some more business points, a short, pudgy man in a neon yellow sweater patted Clint on his shoulders.

"What's good, man, you having fun? Why ya'll talking ova here all serious and shit?"

Clint dapped him up. "B, this is my manager, Luke. Luke, this is B, he's a lawyer."

Luke measured me up, then straightened up quick, still clutching a bottle of Moet like the kids clutched their bottles of formula.

Real professional.

"What's up, Cuz," Luke said, eyes darting between us. "Why you ain't tell me you were coming?"

As I assumed, Clint lacked the proper management. We shook hands.

"I didn't know there was anyone to tell," I said flatly. "An assistant called our firm."

"Assistant? Oh, you mean Jade! That's his girl. Man, she be worrying too much about him. I told her I got everything under control."

Clint gave me a weary look. He wasn't too pleased with his management either.

He's gonna need more help than I thought.

As Luke tried to convince me of his management capabilities, I suppressed a yawn. I grew up drinking and clubbing with half the defensive linemen on the New England Patriots and was used to the party life. But the only late nights I've had in the past year were spent staying up feeding infants. Juggling them all day was exhausting, and I found myself passed out by nine-thirty like an old man. My body wasn't ready to return to my bachelor lifestyle. My mind wasn't sold yet either.

Knowing Clint's pseudo-manager would be latched to us for the rest of the night, it seemed like an opportune time to make a graceful exit without looking like a punk. But, before I sat my glass down, the club lights came on, blinding me as the DJ gave a last call for alcohol.

Real talk, I was relieved the night was over just so I could head back to my hotel. I'm not a lightweight but the Patron shots were hitting me pretty heavy. I approached Clint, surrounded by a group of grown men dressed like college freshman.

"Clint, it was great meeting you. So I'll see tomorrow?"

"Whoa, whoa, wait a minute!" Clint said laughing, patting me on the shoulder. "The night's still young! Why don't you come for a ride with us?"

An hour later, Clint pulled his souped-up truck to Stage Door, an infamous strip club in East Baltimore. The bass of the house music slammed on my eardrums as we walked through the musty smelling crowd to our table in near darkness. The stage was lit with black lights as men ogled over the booty poppers dressed in neon string sets and high heel platforms, glowing like psychedelic stars. Their faces were invisible under their bright neon wigs, but irrelevant since their faces were not nearly as important as their bodies.

"Aight kids, let's make 'em work for their money," Clint said, rubbing his palms together with a smirk.

As we sat by the stage, a waitress brought three bottles of Grey Goose and two bottles of Patron on ice to the table. Clint smiled and tipped her.

Hmmm… must be a regular.

The manager approached our table next with a greedy smile. They exchanged a few words, then he handed Clint three thick wads of cash.

"Here you go." Clint tossed me a wad of single dollar bills, at least a thousand dollars' worth. I gripped the wad of cash as Clint and his boys threw money in the air.

What a fucking waste. I'd rather give this to a heroin addict than one of these crusty bitches.

Two girls were on the stage, one in a long, hot pink wig. The other, a short lime-green bob. They bent and touched their toes, wiggling their large asses in front of Clint. Pink hair jumped up on a pole then slide back down in a porn-worthy split that made the boys jump.

"Ohhhhhhh!"

They cheered, captivated by the broad, like children at a circus. They showered the girls with bills, covering the stage floor like snow. Strippers were entertaining at best, but not particularly enticing. I could never respect a woman who made her living off fooling weak-minded men into spending their hard-earned paychecks just because they could pop their pussy the right way.

Sitting behind them, I sipped on the Patron Clint kept offering me while the night's alcohol soaked further into my blood stream.

I'll let him have his fun. Tomorrow, I'm all business.

But six shots later, I couldn't stop staring. The dancers were mesmerizing, especially Green Hair. The curves on her body, the way the sweat moistened her skin, leaving it glistening and tantalizing. Green Hair glided across the stage on her knees and made her booty clap and my dick got hard. I wondered if I installed a pole would Alexandria do that for me?

Wait a minute, am I really thinking about my wife in a fucking strip club?

Aight, I'll admit. I love Alexandria's body, before the kids and after. Something about how soft her skin was, both inside and out. From the first time I saw her, all I wanted to do was squeeze her thighs and suck on her neck.

"Yo, ladies, you ain't taking care of my man back here," Clint says to Pink Hair, as he slapped a couple of bills on her ample ass. She glanced over at me with a smirk.

"Why don't he come closer to the stage?"

I shook my head but it felt like it was in slow motion.

"Nah, I'm good right here," I said, careful not to slur.

"What's wrong? You afraid of a little pussy," Clint said as his boys cracked up. I was glad they couldn't see my face because I wasn't amused.

Are they serious? This shit ain't nothing for me.

I stood, slowly making my way closer to the stage.

"There's my man!" Clint cheered, making room for me.

The flashing disco lights bounced off the girls' dark skin. My legs were a tad bit looser than they should have been.

"Hey, baby," Pink Hair said, shoving her double–Ds in my face. Someone put a glass in my hand and I kept sipping. She stepped up and grabbed the pole, winding her waist down to the floor. I rocked on my heels, watching the show.

"Excuse me," I said, interrupting her focus. She glanced down at me with a wicked smile.

I pulled out the stack of bills and Pink Hair's eyes lit up—had her full attention now. Green Hair's back was still to me, concentrating on her pole moves.

Pink Hair stopped and squatted in front of me, the glitter sparkling off her chest.

"What's your name, beautiful?" I asked.

"I'm Taylor Made and that's Sasha."

I laughed, composure lost. "Sasha? Ha, that's my dog's name."

"Oooo," she cooed. "Well, is she a bad bitch like Sasha?"

I nodded.

"Well then, let me let Sasha show you just how bad she can be while I take care of your friend." Taylor Made was smart, letting her friend entertain me while she went for Clint and his bigger pockets.

"Sasha! Come over here," she called over her shoulder. "I want you to meet somebody."

Sasha, still jiggling on the pole, began to stride over but stopped as if she had run into an invisible wall. Her body went rigid, trembling.

"Damn," Clint mumbled. "What's her problem?"

I couldn't see her face, but something had clearly spooked her. I strained to see through the darkness and blinding strobe lights as she inched backwards. A red spot-light bounced off her face for a split second. My mouth dropped as the glass slipped out my hand.

"Rachel?"

The sound of her own name made her jump.

Oh shit! It really is her!

We stood frozen, staring at each other. Past the green bob, blue contacts, sparkling chest and makeup, she was almost unrecognizable. She gasped then spun around, racing off stage as fast as her platforms would carry her.

"You know her?" Clint asked, before his boys howled with laughter.

"Oh shit, Mr. Serious been fucking with a stripper," Luke said.

I pushed through them, rushing over to the side of the stage.

"Rachel!" I screamed, following her. She ignored me, passing the other dancers on stage who were confused by her abrupt exit. "Rachel!"

"That's not my name," she snapped.

"Rachel Ebony Davis is your fucking name. Come here now!" I grabbed her by the wrist, yoking her back, but I must have crossed some invisible line because within seconds some 6'7 linebacker jumped up and slammed me into the wall. He pinned my arm back, positioned to snap it in two and for a brief moment I wondered how I was going to explain this to Alexandria.

"Yo, get the fuck off me," I barked, just as Rachel touched the bouncer's shoulder.

"It's alright, Jacks! It's all right."

Jacks nodded his thick head and released my arm, leaving it throbbing. I played it cool, though.

"Meet me by the bar," she sighed in defeat. "I'll be right out."

Rachel disappeared backstage and Jacks stared me down, standing in the way of me following her. I straightened my shirt and headed to the bar. Smoke swirled around my head while the music thumped at my temple. The funk of two decades worth of sweat and sperm crept up from the carpet, invading my nostrils. Clint and his boys were still lavishing Taylor Made with attention.

She'll make at least two grand easy. Wonder how much Rachel's made tonight?

Rachel—my ex-girlfriend, the supposed love of my life, was nothing more than a go-go dancer. I met her my sophomore year of undergrad, where we were both poli-sci majors. Back then, Rachel was gorgeous, brilliant, and determined. Nothing like girls I knew back in Boston. She sat two seats ahead of me in almost every class, raised her hand for every question, and even challenged our Professors. It was fucking sexy. I had to make her mine. Her family lived in California and owned a chain of high-class restaurants, so she came from money, while I was working three jobs trying to make it through school and support Ma at the same time.

For the most part, I kept Rachel in the dark about my former self. She was so sweet and innocent; I didn't want to expose her to that life. Through the years, she was supportive of all my endeavors, especially through my admissions process for law school. After graduation, I landed a full-time job at an advertising firm and formed my real estate company, and we moved in together. Not only was I working during the day and attending law school at night, weekends were jammed packed with studying and flipping proprieties. It left me with little-to-no time for Rachel, who couldn't land a job or internship in the public sector to save her life.

Things started to change between us right away. She wasn't used to not getting what she wanted. As a result, she took her frustrations out on me. I tried to help her every way I could: introduced her to a slew of people she never followed up with, sent her dozens of invites to networking events she never attended, and even managed to hook her up with an interview as an executive assistant for one of my clients. She never showed up, felt the job was beneath her. Her audacity was mind-blowing. I'd been working every day since I was nine. No job was beneath me when I had none. I started to question if she was the right woman to spend the rest of my life with, especially if she couldn't manage to keep it together when life got a little rough. But we had so much history, seemed too late to turn back. And what kind of dick would I have been breaking up with a chick that had been there for me, just because she was down on her luck?

But all her free time gave her ample time to nitpick at our relationship. She became needy, controlling, and insecure to the point of insanity. The arguing was exhausting.

And then came Alexandria…

"What are you doing here?" Rachel asked behind me.

I laughed. "The real question is what are *you* doing here?"

"You still don't know how to answer a question I see."

I bit my tongue and turned, stunned by her appearance. Her breasts were sagging, her skin was covered in thick makeup, and Hefty bags sat under her eyes. But her ass still held its rounded shape and bounce. I marveled at my handiwork, knowing years of my backstrokes help put that ass there.

Rachel slid onto the stool beside me. She had put on a sheer, bright orange cover up that didn't cover much. When we dated, it was like pulling teeth trying to make her wear lingerie. I practically had to beg her to wear a thong from time to time. She was always Miss Prim and Proper.

"Your cousin told me you moved to Atlanta," she said.

"I did. Looks like you moved, too."

"D.C. to Baltimore isn't exactly a huge move," she chuckled.

"Did your job help you with the relocation fees?" I smirked and knocked back the Patron.

Damn, Ma would be so disappointed in her.

From the first time they met, Ma loved Rachel. She considered her a part of the family, even after we broke up. Once, after we'd ended it, I came home for Christmas and found Rachel sitting in our living room. I stayed at a hotel that year.

Rachel rolled her eyes and ordered a double shot of Hennessey. She never used to drink. Just as I was about to ask more questions, the manager swooped in.

"Aye, shouldn't you be on stage?"

Rachel tensed up and began to stutter some excuses. I tossed the wad of cash on the counter. "Here. That should cover her time."

The manager paused for a beat then nodded, giving her a warning glare before walking back to his office. Rachel's shoulders eased with a long exhale.

"Thanks. Dude is always breathing down my back. Shit."

She curses now too. It was almost too much.

"Damn, Rachel… what happened to you?"

"What'd you mean?" she said, as if we weren't talking in the middle of a cesspool.

Knowing how high strung and sensitive she could be, I tried to choose my words but it was difficult in my drunken stupor. "I mean, what the fuck are you doing working in a place like this?"

She shrugged as if it were no big deal to be one step up from a hooker. "Well, a girl's gotta pay the bills," she said with a huff, squaring her shoulders.

I stopped keeping track of Rachel once I moved to Atlanta, but last I heard she had become a bit of a chickenhead, sleeping with any dude she could get her hands on, especially ones I knew, almost deliberately. Maybe she thought it would spur some type of reaction out of me. I thought it was just a passing phase, not a lifestyle choice.

"Rachel, you could've been anything you wanted. Anything but this. This… is not you."

"How do you know?" she snapped.

"I know you."

"Oh, really?" she chuckled. "Well I thought I knew you too. But I was wrong about that, wasn't I?"

Figures. Of course she would blame this on me.

"Rachel, we were having our own set of problems and—"

"That's some bullshit! So what, we were having problems? That doesn't give you the excuse to fuck some other bitch. Alex? That was her name, right?" She laughed. I used to love her laugh, now the sound revolted me. "What's fucked up is that she knew about me," she barked. "She *knew*. And you *knew*, yet you still fucked her."

Her voice was rising unnecessarily. And for some reason, I felt the need to defend Alexandria.

"There's no need to bring her into this. You knew I was already one foot out the door when it happened. We hadn't been 'us' in quite some time before she came into the picture."

"Yeah, but she was sure there to seal the deal, right? Now, let me think, what was the best line in that letter? Oh yeah! The part where she said 'it's either her or me'. Guess you chose her, huh?" She scoffed and shot back her drink while I held my composure.

That stupid fucking letter!

In one of her meager attempts to break things off between us, Alexandria wrote a scathing email, detailing all the particulars of our relationship faults followed by an ultimatum. Rachel, being Rachel, found the email. *Caught.* If Alexandria had never written that damn letter, Rachel wouldn't have ever known a thing. I had no idea how she figured out the password to my email account but she had crossed a line. I wasn't a fan of invasion of privacy.

"You shouldn't have been snooping around my personal effects," I said in an even tone.

Rachel's eyes blazed open. "Fuck you! I had a right to know why, all of a sudden, you wanted to break up with me!"

"So the reasons I supplied weren't adequate enough that you resorted to hacking and cyber stalking?"

"You blindsided me," she stuttered. "You lied!"

"For the last time, it wasn't all of a sudden. We were having problems, you couldn't have been that dense not to recognize that."

She tore her eyes away from me and ordered another drink. She was petulant, but for the wrong reasons. I didn't choose Alexandria over Rachel. I choose freedom. It wasn't Alexandria's ultimatum that made me change, it was my own.

Should I stay in an unhealthy relationship or go?

"You thought you were so smart," she hissed. "So fucking slick. Smooth, that's what they use to call you, right? Well, I caught your mother-fucking smooth ass in a lie!" Rachel finished her drink in one gulp. "You swore you'd never cheat on me! You said you hated cheaters. But you were one. You always were! How many girls were there before Alex?"

I groaned, rubbing my temple. She was plucking my last nerve with her delusional thoughts. I was loyal to her. I put up with her emotional roller coaster for four years. I deserved a purple heart for making it out of that relationship without trying to cut off my own ears to keep from hearing her whining. Complaining about not getting the job she wanted. Crying about the trips and clothes she couldn't afford to go on. Nagging about the lack of time I had for her because of law school. She even went as far as to say that she didn't think she could handle me being in law school and that I needed to decide what was more important: her or my education.

Thinking back on all her issues makes Alexandria's tantrums mere hiccups rather than earthquakes. At least her tantrums were somewhat warranted. But I supposed Rachel deserved some honesty.

"Yeah, it was fucked up, what I did to you," I relented. "But… it is what it is. You didn't have to throw your whole life away because of it. We weren't going to work out and you knew that!"

She shook her head. "You think I'm working here because of you? Ha! You were always a cocky bastard. You don't know nothing."

She ordered another drink, swaying like a lush. "Fucking asshole," she mumbled into her glass.

"I see your communications skills have not improved."

"Fuck you," she slurred. The waitress gave me a wary glance as she mopped up the spilled alcohol Rachel sloshed on the counter.

She couldn't have gotten this drunk that fast.

I checked her arms for track marks, then her eyes. Her pupils were dilated

Maybe pills? Ecstasy? Xanax? What are people using nowadays?

Then that feeling came back again, something in between guilt and pity. No matter how we left off, Rachel was better than this. She needed help. I stood, gently pulling her arm towards the exit, ready to be her knight-in-shining-armor, ready to rescue her from herself. She had no idea what she had gotten herself into. Her naivety was always her downfall.

"Come on. Let me take you home."

"Hell no! Get off of me, don't touch me," she screamed, slapping my hand away, punching my arm as if I was trying to rape her. She barely left a scratch yet her audacity struck me blind.

She's a fucking psychopath.

I sat down back down and the guilt I felt quickly vanished.

"We were special, Braxton," Rachel whined palming her drink. "We had something special. And you threw it all away for what? Where's your precious fucking Alexandria now?"

She didn't know.

I smirked as I turned back to my glass and said something I wouldn't have normally said if I were sober. "She is in our home. With our children."

The club went silent for a fraction of a second before a tidal wave of alcohol splashed in my face. I rubbed my eyes dry and turned to Rachel, prepared to yoke her up by her neck, but too angry to move. Her nostrils flared, eyes raving mad as her entire body trembled in rage. She threw the glass down by her feet and it shattered on the carpet.

"Yo! What the fuck!" I heard Clint scream, running to my side. Rachel turned on her heels and stormed away, crunching over the glass. I could have wrung my shirt out over a cup. The bartender, amused, passed me a few napkins.

"You alright?" Clint asked, patting me on the back as if to say "good game."

"Yeah, I'm straight."

"What the fuck that bitch do that for? You want me to handle this shit? I know the owner."

"Nah man, I'm good. Let her go." There was no sense chasing her down, getting her fired from the only suitable job she could probably muster up. She was 'good girl gone bad' personified, and I supposed I had a part in her demise. I knew she took our break up hard, but to these lengths? The only thing left for me to do was to show some justifiable mercy by leaving her be.

I headed towards the bathroom to dry off, passing the stage—full of Rachels—wondering how many men had driven them there.

Chapter 5

"Man, you are the worst!" my cousin Kevin heckled after I recounted my run in with Rachel. "I can't believe she threw a drink on you, though. That's a first."

"What can I say, the ladies love me," I winced as I chugged more Gatorade, my hangover beating me with a metal bat. We walked into the property that we were trying to unload: an empty three-bedroom town house on the outskirts of Silver Spring, Maryland. Even though Kevin was two inches shorter than me and stocky, we could pass for brothers on some days. The genes in our family were strong.

"Yeah, and what did Regal teach you about the ladies," Kevin laughed, opening a window to air out the staleness in the house.

Regal. Damn, I haven't heard anyone else say his name in years.

When my mother became ill with her last pregnancy and couldn't work, we were down to our last dollar. We couldn't let my family starve, so Brian and I went to work. We sold candy and snacks we stole from the corner store at school during the day, water to the construction workers in the afternoons, and made runs for the hustlers at night. Brian fell in love with the money; I was only doing it to support my family. People started to recognize that I wasn't the average kid on the block and I got a reputation for my no nonsense attitude. Regal, one of the most well-known hustlers in the game, paid special attention to us and eventually took me under his wing. It wasn't long before he started teaching me the "rules."

"My pops taught me these rules," he had said. "Got me where I am today. Live by them little man."

Since Regal was well-respected and connected, and my father didn't bother to teach me anything, I figured his rules must work. So I listened. Brian on the other hand couldn't be bothered.

"Man, I got enough school at school," Brian had said and blew off our afternoon talks. Regal would just wave him off and say, "He'll learn the hard way."

Slowly, Regal started teaching me rules one through ten. Soon, I was using them in every aspect of my life, even when dealing with teachers or girls I had crushes on. I grew up with Regal as a mentor, always protecting me from doing anything stupid or getting too deep into the game. I wasn't always so innocent, though. I had to gun-butt a couple of dudes just to prove a point, but since I was cool with Regal, no one dared to retaliate. Still, I slept with a Beretta under my pillow and kept a .45 in my locker. There was no saving Brian, though.

Right before he was killed, Regal told me there were only three tickets out of the hood: college, prison, or a body bag. So when Regal was gunned down in his own bed by some punk kid trying to prove himself, and Brian was caught on his third strike, college looked more and more like the savvy decision. I often wondered what Regal would've done if he was in my shoes when it came to Alexandria.

"Aye, man, sorry," Kevin said, suddenly serious. "I was just messing around, didn't mean to bring up bad memories."

"Nah, I'm straight," I said, shrugging him off.

"Anyways, thanks for coming through. I thought it'd speed up the process if she met both the owners."

He sat his bag down and pulled out some files. Kevin and I started working in real estate during our senior year in undergrad. We were put on by some old, Jewish Donald Trump-looking dude who convinced us to take his real estate course. He taught us all the tricks to the trade, what classes to take, licenses to get, properties to buy. We made a hundred grand in our first six months.

"So, who are we meeting? You think she's really gonna buy?" I asked, popping some more Advil. She was late and my brain was self-destructing with one of the worst hangovers I remember in recent history.

"She seemed pretty interested."

"What does she do?" She could sell horseshoes and bubble gum for all I cared, as long as she had the down payment. The property was eating away at my pockets. My footsteps echoed in the living room.

Kevin shrugged, flipping through his disheveled piles of paper. "Some sort of writer or something. She's young like us, though. Think she graduated from Howard University." He finally located the scribbled piece of paper in the pile. "Her name is… Tiffany Jackson."

I froze and spun around.

"Wait… what did you just say?" But before he could repeat himself, the door opened.

"Braxton?" Tiffany, stunned, froze in the doorway.

Oh shit.

"Hey… what's up?" I said coolly, racing to compose myself, hoping the floor would cave in or a plane would crash next door.

Tiffany was slender, almost too thin from some angles, with thick black hair that trickled down her long back. Her light skin was sprinkled with light brown freckles. From a distance you would swear she was white.

"What… what are you doing here?" She glanced around the empty home as if she was preparing for a pending attack.

When you're caught in this sort of circumstance, the trick is to make the other person, specifically a female, feel crazy so they won't detect the mini heart attack you are actually having. I feigned a smile. "Trying to sell this old place."

"No… I meant what are you doing in D.C.?" she asked in a low voice, her eyebrow arching.

I didn't respond. Kevin took his cue and crossed the living room to greet her. "I see you two have met. I'm Kevin, we spoke on the phone."

She tore her eyes away from me, finally noticing Kevin. Her deep pink lips parted into a stunning smile accented by dimples. "Kevin, right, nice to meet you. Sorry I'm late, had a late meeting then ran into some traffic on the 495."

"No problem. Please, come on in."

She sashayed across the living room, her hips pronouncing every step. She was wearing a tight light-colored skirt and a matching V-neck. Kevin lingered behind her, checked out her ass, and nodded in approval.

It never occurred to me how much Tiffany favored Alexandria. Enough to make me question if they were distant relatives of some sort. In Alexandria's warped mind, the slave ship made a beeline from Africa to Queens, dropping her family off. Tiffany was also from New York, but her family was from the West Indies. And yet, she had the same bright, childlike eyes as Alexandria. Their hair had the same thickness and length too, but Alexandria lacked Tiffany's grace and flirtatious swag.

"It's good to see you," she said, greeting me with a tight hug around my neck. She smelled like vanilla and cocoa butter. Alexandria always smelled like oranges.

She pulled back, her eyes gazing directly into mine for half a second before stepping back. Her smell lingered, sending a direct message to my dick. I wanted to slam her against a wall and rip that fucking skirt off.

"You never told me you were house hunting," I said, trying to change the subject to something more practical, throwing ice on my nuts.

"Well, if you'd called more often I would have," she said with a smirk. She was good for digs like that.

"Been pretty busy."

"Hmmm... I'm sure." As she turned to admire the house, Kevin threw me a curious glance, mouthing "Alex" at me. I shook my head slowly and he nodded. He wouldn't dare bring up Alex in front of another woman. Guy code states that you never bring up a girlfriend, or wife, in front of a hot chick.

"This is a pretty big house," I said, stepping behind her.

"I know, but I need the room for me and my dog."

Tiffany had an eight-pound Chihuahua named Oscar, the gayest dog in the world. Sasha could use him as a toothpick.

Another difference, unlike Alexandria, Tiffany loved dogs.

"I've seen cats bigger than your dog."

She chuckled and raised an eyebrow. "What he lacks in size he makes up for with personality. Unlike some men I know."

Kevin chuckled and I smirked at him. Like Alexandria, Tiffany also considered herself a comedian.

"Well, it is a lot of space for a single lady. Maybe you could rent out the basement. It's fully renovated," Kevin said as we walked into the adjoining dining room.

"No, thanks. I prefer to live alone, unless, of course, a certain someone decides to move back to D.C. Then I'll need all the space I can get."

She flashed one of those brilliant smiles at me and quickly turned to admire the crown molding. Kevin couldn't stop staring, captivated by her. I felt the same way.

"How about you show me around," she said to Kevin who finally closed his gaping mouth. He gave her a tour of the three bedrooms, the walk-in closet, the master bathroom, the finished basement, and the spacious kitchen with all new stainless steel appliances. I lingered behind them like a stalker, admiring the view. Tiffany took in the details, gazing around and every so often her eyes would land on me. She would smile then continue her observation.

"I heard you were writing a book," I finally said in the last bedroom. She nodded without glancing at me as she opened the closet doors. "Hope it's not about me." I was only half joking.

Her laugh echoed and bounced off the walls in the empty room.

"Maybe it will be, you never know, you're a pretty interesting character. But I promise, I'll change the name to Bernard or Brandon, so as not to give away your true identity. Bond. James Bond. Man of Mystery."

She smiled and followed Kevin back downstairs.

The three of us walked out onto the sunny patio deck. You could smell spring in the air. Tiffany admired the narrow backyard, enclosed by a white picket fence and a few tall trees.

"Oscar would love this. It's the perfect place for him to lie out. He loves the sun." She spun around and nodded. "I love it. Although, are you pretty set on the asking price?"

I felt Kevin's eyes burning a hole in my neck and I shrugged.

"We may be able to work something out." Kevin shook his head softly, disapproving. We had already knocked the price down considerably given the bad market. Any more and we'd barely make a profit.

"Well, how about we discuss this over some drinks? Plus, it'll give us a chance to catch up. Seeing how you decided to come into town and not say anything."

Kevin raised an eyebrow and stepped away, his silent judgment evident. But it's not like I had reached out to the girl the moment my plane landed. I had made a valid effort to keep out of trouble by not contacting Tiffany, but trouble found me instead. Plus, we were only going to talk business about the house, nothing wrong with that. Alexandria seeped into my thoughts and I shook her away quickly.

No harm in getting a drink with an old friend.

"Fair enough, drinks it is."

***

I sat at a small table in the virtually empty bar of the Marriot hotel by the Capital. Kevin didn't say much on our ride back to the hotel, except to mumble something about drawing up the contract for the sale before dropping me off. After checking in with Sharlene, I took a quick shower to freshen up, and headed to the bar.

Tiffany was punctual. Facing the door, I waited with a glass of red wine. Not my usual taste, but I needed to start off light. I was still suffering from last night's migraine and was ready to put my head in a freezer. A cocktail waitress approached my table just as Tiffany stepped in. She had changed into a navy blue wrap dress and red heels with a fresh coat of red lipstick. She stood by the door for a moment then smiled when she spotted me. Her smile lit up the room and caught the attention of every wayward traveling businessman in the place. She rushed over to the table and I stood to greet her.

"Hi!" she squeaked and kissed my cheek for a fraction of second too long, before sitting down and grabbing the drink menu. Her hair grazed my cheek, the scent sticking in my nose. I wondered what it would be like pulling her hair as she arched her back and cocked her ass up for me.

"I'll start with a chocolate martini, please," she said quickly to the waitress and turned to me with a satisfied sigh.

"This place has the best martinis," she said as she shrugged out of her cardigan, revealing her glowing shoulders and collarbone. I caught myself staring like a fucking teenager and averted my eyes. She grinned and fluffed her hair some. Tiffany was completely aware of her beauty, but not cocky about it, merely using it as a way of demanding the attention in a room full of men.

Another difference. Alexandria was completely oblivious of her beauty—it was almost frustrating. To watch men ogle at her as we walked through Lenox mall, even when she was pushing a double wide stroller, drove me fucking insane. Probably why I kept Alexandria hidden for so long. Keeping her in the house was the only way to avoid manslaughter charges. But I would never admit that to anyone.

"So... what's new with you?" she asked, and I pushed Alexandria to the back of my mind.

"I was about to ask you the same thing. House? Book?"

She smiled. "Yeah, I guess I've been pretty busy. But you still haven't answered my question."

"I've been pretty busy as well."

"We've covered that. But what brings you to D.C.? And more importantly, why didn't you tell me?" She wasn't pushy, but for some reason, it was hard to dodge her questions. She had a great memory.

"I had business with a new client. Plus, I figured I'd surprise you."

She chuckled as the waitress returned with her drink.

"That's pretty bold of you. What if you had just showed up at my place, how would you know some other dude wasn't going to be there?"

I laughed at the thought—I never went to woman's place uninvited. But Tiffany was fairly predictable. There was no other man. Or no other man she was interested in. She was the equivalent to a dude, the chase turned her on.

"I'd tell dude to excuse us for a moment."

She giggled and sipped her drink, glancing at my left hand.

"Ok, I see no ring mark, so it's safe to assume you're still unhitched."

I stopped breathing but kept an even face. "If that's what you think."

She nodded and glanced around the bar. "So how long are you in town for?"

"Just a couple of days."

"Pity," she pouted, twirling her hair around her finger. "And about the place..."

"Ah, yes, the place."

"I was hoping we could maybe work something out." Her seductive smile would distract a weaker man. I straighten up in my chair, preparing to debate.

"Well, you know the asking price is pretty fair."

She scoffed. "In this market? Please. I could get the same house in the same area for at least five thousand less, plus the owner would pay half of my closing costs."

Damn, she knows her shit.

"So is that what you want?" I asked.

Her mischievous smile curved to her glass. "That's not all I want."

I shifted in my seat. The room was starting to heat up.

Maybe we'd be more comfortable in my room.

It took some effort but I shook the thought out of my head. I was here for business. I needed to remember that before this temptress got the better of me. We ordered another round of drinks and discussed the property for a bit longer. She was ecstatic and eager about the opportunity. I was sure I had sealed the deal.

"So I guess once we sign the paperwork, we can celebrate," she said, her eyes searching my face, biting her lower lip.

I want to celebrate right here on this table.

Just then, my Blackberry vibrated, an urgent message from Sharlene.

"Damn, sorry, I have to go. Being called into an emergency conference call with my boss."

"Well, that sucks," she said with a pout. "Tell you what, since you're in town, why don't you come over for dinner tomorrow night?"

Uh-oh.

"You don't know how to cook," I teased, trying to dodge her sticky invitation. She flipped her hair back, grabbed her purse, took out a twenty, and placed it on the table. Her independence turned me on—almost blew a nut right under the table.

"Ha! That's what you think," she giggled.

I shrugged. "Well… I'm not sure. Maybe."

"Well think about it. You have a couple of days. It's an open invitation," she said and stood up with a bounce. "I'll walk you to your room."

Shit.

"You don't have to do that," I said, imagining the positions I'd contort her body in if she came within a foot of my door.

She smiled. "I know."

As we walked towards my room in silence, I tried to find a way to convince her not to come in without hurting my chances with her.

My chances? Damn, what the hell am I doing?

We stopped at my door and stood in uncomfortable silence.

"So this is you, huh?" she asked, her cheeks flushing pink.

"Yep, this is me," I said, playing with the key card in my pocket.

She bit the bottom of her lip as she glanced around the hall, and I had the distinct feeling she was waiting for an invitation.

Maybe it won't be so bad… to let an old friend hang in my room. Just for a little while.

But my buzzing phone thwarted that plan.

"Well, I have to… jump on this conference call now."

Her face darkened as her lip puckered into a small pout. I wanted to fuck her mouth into the middle of next week.

"So… I guess… dinner at your place," I said. "Tomorrow, right?"

She smiled and wrapped her whole body around me in a tight hug, pushing her tits into my chest. Her hair tickled my nose. Her plump lips sucked on my cheek, I could've sworn I felt tongue. She let go with a satisfied grin and strolled away, looking over her shoulder.

"Tomorrow."

I closed the door and never wanted a cold shower so fucking badly in my entire life. But Sharlene was patching me into a call with Mr. Paul.

"Braxton!" he cheered. "How's it going so far?"

"So far so good, sir," I said, popping two more aspirin for my suffering blue balls and swollen dick.

"So, how's it looking with Clint?"

"It's… progressing. We've made some headway. I feel confident about the potential."

"Ok," he said skeptically. "Well, I'm counting on you to bring this home for us. We need him signed within the week. If you think you need some back up, I'll be happy to send–"

"That won't be necessary, sir," I said, keeping my tone level. "The deal is as good as done."

***

Another sleepless night, but at least this time it was from my own affliction and not partying with Clint. Drinks with Tiffany had me restless. One part of me wanted to pull her inside, fuck her on every square inch of my hotel room. The other part couldn't understand why I was hesitating. The ink on my marriage license was barely dry, and it wasn't like I was completely lost in the throes of matrimony. Plus, we were married out of practicality. There was no need to give up my identity just yet. *Right?*

I flipped through the TV channels, annoyed by the lack of late-night programming.

If Alexandria was here, she'd probably find something for us to watch. She's good at that.

My eyes wouldn't allow my body to rest, and the bed was freezing, even though I had turned the heat up. I rubbed the shaft of my dick.

If Alexandria was here…

Alexandria kept our bed the perfect temperature. Her body was my own personal space heater. I had laid a couple of pillows sideways, trying to simulate her presence. But the pillows didn't have her scent. Or her adorable snore.

I'm being a real pussy, missing my woman like this, but fuck it.

With a sigh of defeat, I picked up the phone and dialed.

"Hello?" A sleep-deprived voice answered after the fifth ring.

"You awake? What are you doing?"

"Oh, nothing important, just sleeping," she grumbled. "It's only three in the damn morning."

I missed her sarcasm too.

"Oh good, glad I caught you."

She grunted. "What's wrong?"

"Nothing. Why something gotta be wrong?"

"'Cause you're calling me in the middle of the night," she groaned.

"How are the kids?" I asked, ignoring her tone.

"Well, they're maintaining a balance of crazy cuteness and utter madness."

"Doing their Daddy proud, I see."

"Beth started walking."

It was like she sucker punched me, right in the gut. Never had I been so thankful Alexandria couldn't see my face. "What?" I asked, unable to hide my complete disbelief.

"Yeah, she started walking, finally. I knew she was going to be the first."

"Wow... she's... walking?"

"Yeah. It was pretty cool..."

As Alexandria recounted the story of my baby girl, my first born (technically speaking) stumbling across the living floor, jealousy consumed me. I wasn't there. I had seen all her first moments—first time she rolled over, first time she crawled, her first word: Mama.

How could I miss her most important first?

"Braxton? Braxton? You there?"

"Yeah. I'm here," I said, trying to shake the raging disappointment out of my voice before Alexandria noticed.

I've only been gone three days! How could I miss so much?

"Well... that's nice," I said flatly. "So, what else have you been up to?"

"Braxton, what's wrong with you? Did someone die?"

This woman!

"Damn, can't I call just to see how you're doing," I snapped.

Crickets. "Oh. My. God! You miss me, don't you? Ha!"

"I didn't say that."

Alexandria laughed so hard she snorted. "Well, well, well. Look at that! The stone cold Braxton Earwood missing someone. Awww, baby!"

"Cut it out. And don't call me baby."

"Alright, alright, fine," her laughter dying down. "I miss you, too."

The bed finally warmed up and once again I found myself grateful she wasn't with me, or she would have seen the big cheese ball smile that grew across my face. No one had the ability to make me laugh like she did. I craved her ridiculousness, her insanity, her smartass mouth. I craved her.

"Soooo... what are you wearing?"

She laughed. "Are you serious?"

"What?" I asked innocently. "I'm just asking a question."

"Ha! You really want to do this?"

I shrugged as if she could see me. "I'm just curious."

She paused for a beat, then said, "I'm wearing your law school t-shirt."

"Hmmm…what else?"

"Absolutely nothing," she cooed, and the thought of my t-shirt hugging her ass made the bed hotter. "What are you wearing?"

I tossed back the comforter. "Boxer briefs—red ones."

"Mmm… my favorite. I love you in red."

Her voice was so sexy, just the way she whispered. The bed was burning up. "Damn, it's pretty hot. Maybe you should take off that t-shirt. Wouldn't want you to get heat stroke."

She giggled and I heard the phone ruffle around a bit.

"Ok. It's off now," she said with a sigh. "Thanks, I feel freer now."

The thought of her completely naked, in my bed, with that grin that made me want to blow her back out… I almost booked a flight back home. I slipped a hand down my boxers.

"Hey, can you do something for me?" I asked.

"Sure. Anything," she moaned.

"I want you to imagine me, fucking you. Not some love-making shit. I want to tease you until you're begging me to fuck you."

"Mmm… that's easy. I do that all the time."

She does? Wow.

"Ha. Well maybe this time I can help you out and make it a bit more real. How about you take your right hand, starting from that spot right behind your ear, and slide it down slow, until I tell you to stop. Can you do that for me?"

"Uh-huh," she whispered.

"Good girl. Now, close your eyes and start. Remember, *slowly.*" I waited a few moments, picturing her naked body, her back arching for me. "Alexandria, tell me where your hand is right now."

For a moment, she was silent. Then she says, "It's on my collar bone."

"Mmmm, I love your collarbone. It's so sexy and sweet. I love the way it tastes. Continue."

"What are you doing?" she asked.

"I'm stroking my dick."

"My dick," she corrected and I could practically hear her grin through the phone.

I chuckle. "You can have it, if you're a good girl and listen. Where is your hand now?"

She swallows. "On my nipple."

"The right one or the left one?"

"The right one," she gasped.

"Mmmm… my favorite. I love the way it feels between my lips, the way it tastes. Pinch it."

She whimpered slightly and I sat up, noticing the pre-cum on my hand.

"Harder, Alexandria, twist it just slightly," I ordered and she whimpered again.

"Do the other one. I love the way that one tastes, too."

"Braxton," she pants. "Can I keep going?"

"What's the rush? I like to take my time," I teased.

She whimpered again.

"Ok, you can keep going now Alexandria."

Between her panting and my strokes, I was about to blow a load in my hotel sheets.

Fuck, I miss her. Fuck, I want her.

"Where is your hand now Alexandria?" I asked, groaning.

"My… my… pussy," she said, struggling with the naughty word. I grinned.

"Oh that, I definitely, DEFINITELY love the way that tastes. Do you want me to taste it?"

"Yes," she moaned, almost like a cry.

"How badly do you want me to taste it?"

"Really, really badly," she begged. I loved the way she used to beg me for more when I was on top of her, stroking her until her body would writhe, and still she'd scream for more. Slamming deeper into her, fisting her breasts, taking out all my aggression on her body. She took it and she loved it.

The air was getting hot and thick in my hotel room, and I knew I wasn't going to be able to hold on for much longer. But I had to, because I fucking loved the noise she made when she came.

"Is it mine?" I asked eagerly.

"Yes, it's yours," she panted.

"You sure about that?"

"Yes, yes. It's most definitely yours."

"Good. Now, add another finger. "

"Ah," she panted. "Ohhhh… I… think I'm…"

"No! Not yet," I growled. "I didn't say yet."

"But I'm... I can't... please..."

Ha! The magic word.

"Say that again," I growled.

"Please... please... please... Ahhhh."

My head started to go numb. I closed my eyes and pictured her face. Her eyes gazing up at me, her tits all thick and round in my face. I squeezed my junk tighter, to match her tight pussy.

Shit, I haven't jerked off like this since high school.

"Fuck, Alex!" I coughed out, and I let out some type of indistinguishable noise before falling back on the bed, lightheaded and out of breath. Gasping for air, I grabbed a napkin off my room service cart, dropping the phone in the process. From a distance I heard her moan break into a scream and she called my name. Even from states away, the sound made me horny all over again.

***

"I think Ma's sick," my baby sister Paris said over the phone, her childlike voice matching her petite frame and demeanor.

"What do you mean? What's wrong?"

I had just finished up a meeting with Dante Jergans and his manager. A grueling five hour lunch at District Grill, going over and over again the key terms in his new agreement. Dante wasn't the sharpest tool in the shed. Back at the hotel, I jumped in the shower and was getting ready to have dinner with Clint—without his annoying manager. If everything went smoothly, I'd be able to lock the deal and catch an early flight back home to Alexandria and the kids.

That was the plan until my sister called me.

"I don't know," Paris said. "She's just not feeling good."

"She didn't say anything to me about it," I said just as there was a knock on my suite door. The concierge swooped in with my freshly pressed shirt and slacks. I tipped him before he left.

"Well, you know Ma," Paris said. "She ain't gonna tell you when something's wrong. But she's been extra tired, staying in her bed a lot. She barely cooks, she don't eat and she won't go to the doctor. Something's wrong."

That was strange. Ma cooked everyday as if she was feeding the New England Patriots' starting line-up, even if there were only two people in the house.

"I'll call her today," I said as a text dinged. A message from Tiffany.

Hey there. What time are you coming tonight?

Shit! I forgot about dinner.

"Also," Paris said hesitantly. "I didn't want to tell you this… but… Brian is coming home tomorrow."

"What? I thought he didn't get out until next month?"

"He called this morning."

Shit.

I let out a heavy sigh, dug my bag out of the bottom of the closet and started to pack.

"I'm on my way."

"Are you sure? What about Alex?"

"I'll figure something out."

CHAPTER 6

"I can't believe you married that bitch!"

"Can I get in the car first before you start to chastise me," I said through the open car window.

Nina, parked in front of the arrival terminal at Logan International Airport, rolled her hazel eyes and unlocked the jeep doors. She had those long blond extensions I hated, and a new nose ring.

"Ma just told me," she snapped.

"I'm not surprised."

"You're a fucking dumb ass!"

I grinned and jumped in before she sped off. "Good to see you too, Sis."

Nina wasn't the biggest fan of Alexandria and appointed herself the leader of the gold diggers witch hunt. She believed, and still believes, Alexandria impregnated herself.

"Why would you do something so stupid?" she asked as she cut off two cars switching lanes. I buckled my seat belt.

"You wouldn't understand."

"What... you love her or something?" Her face turned up as if she smelled something rotting. Her revulsion of the idea was hilarious.

"She's tolerable. Besides, it was more of a business decision."

"Yeah, and I bet you she thought the same thing when she got herself knocked up."

I sighed. "Whatever you say."

When I found out Alexandria was pregnant, I had done my due diligence to be certain the kids were mine. I consulted with several doctors, even paid Dr. Turner under the table to do blood tests once the babies were born—without Alexandria knowing. Everyone concluded it was a natural pregnancy, but the truth was, I always just *knew*, felt it from the very beginning. Plus,

Alexandria didn't want to be pregnant as much as I didn't want her to be. It's safe to say she had no interest in being a mother. She was career-driven, had a tenacity that I didn't see in many women. She wouldn't have given up her independence so willingly. But not even Jesus himself could convince Nina of that fact.

The ground surrounding the highway was covered in snow, a solid block of ice, at least two feet deep. Boston could look and feel like Antarctica during winter. Alexandria was not thrilled with the last minute detour, extending my trip another three days. But it wasn't open for discussion. There was a family emergency. I needed to be home.

"How are the kids?" Nina asked, her tone softening.

"They're well."

"Are they walking yet?"

"Beth just started," I mumbled, not wanting to talk about it. "And how are your kids?"

"They're with their father," she sighed. "If I had known you were coming, I would have asked to have them this weekend."

Nina had two girls, one born when she was just sixteen. She lost full custody of them after a DWI incident I could not get her out of.

We pulled up to the old house and I winced at the sight of it. As much money as I put into fixing it, it still looked beaten and broken from the outside. Perhaps it was the surrounding, equally bent-out-of-shape houses that made it appear that way. Ma refused to let me buy her a new crib, refused to be moved.

"Ma?" Nina called as we walked in, and threw her keys on the side table while I did a quick inspection. The paint job that I paid for in the living room looked pretty good; a cheerful coral. The new L-shaped leather sofa looked comfortable. And that new flat screen, mounted above the fireplace, looked as good as it did in the store. The house still smelled of Ma: Pink oil and coffee grinds.

"Ma? Where is everybody? Why is it so quiet in here," Nina said, shaking out her coat. Her jeans and sweater looked extra tight on her.

I hope she's just getting fat and not pregnant again.

We walked through the dark wood panel hallway towards the kitchen where the walls were covered with family portraits. My favorite: a picture of us after my law school graduation ceremony. The only person missing was my brother. He had been locked up for a gun charge. A stupid move, letting the police search his car without probable cause, but Brian was the captain of piss poor decisions, as Alexandria would say.

I had ordered Ma new stainless steel appliances and expected to find them installed and functional, but I found an even bigger surprise waiting in the kitchen.

"Well, look who it is!" Ma exclaimed, sitting at the kitchen table with a cup of tea. Paris was right, she did look weak. She hadn't looked so fragile since the last time she was pregnant. I had to compose my face to keep from reacting because the person sitting next to her was equally as alarming. Brian rose from his seat with a sly grin.

"What's up," he said and I almost didn't recognize his voice. It had been years.

"Oh my God!" Nina shouted happily and jumped into his arms. "I can't believe you're home!"

Brian never took his eyes off me as his sly grin grew.

What are you up to now?

"Good to see you, B."

***

After a huge welcome home dinner, Brian, Paris, and Nina hung out in the living room, retelling stories and cracking jokes while I finished my sweet potato pie in the kitchen with Ma.

I'll have to hit the gym twice as hard when I get back after all this.

"He still looks like your twin," Ma said laughing, loading the last dishes into the new dishwasher I had installed. Brian looked like the corn-rowed, tattooed version of me. There were times that people couldn't tell us apart. But Brian's loud and outgoing personality was always his tell.

"He's lost so much weight though. That place sure don't feed them good," she continued as she stuffed the leftovers in the fridge and wiped her damp hands on a dishtowel. "Everyone makes mistakes. They don't need to starve folks as punishment." She acted as if he was just coming back from summer camp, rather than a five-year sentence at a federal penitentiary.

Ma stayed devoted to Brian through all his transgressions. No matter how many mistakes he made, and there were many, she always welcomed him back with open arms. Regardless of the stores he robbed, the pounds of coke he was found with, or the gun charges he faced, he was a saint in her eyes.

The teapot whistled and Ma moved about the kitchen, sluggish and slow. There was something different about her, besides the few extra strands of gray and the weight loss. She was quiet and had barely touched her plate at dinner.

"I suppose I should go to the store. Not used to having all my children under one roof with me." She smiled at that thought while pouring herself another cup of tea.

"I'll go to the store for you, Ma."

"You don't know what to get dear," she said, shaking her head.

"Make a list. I'll figure it out. I do it all the time for Alexandria."

"Oh, that reminds me," she said, sitting at the table with me. "I have to call Alex and add a few more people to the guest list. Your Uncle Sam and his wife are going to come to the christening. And your cousin Eric made the invitations. Those colors Alex picked were just all wrong. Poor chile don't know no better."

I grinned.

Ha! I'm sure Alexandria will love that.

"Speaking of Alex, I don't suppose I could be planning a REAL wedding anytime soon?" Ma was furious about our quickie Justice of the Peace ceremony. It took me an hour to convince her it was just a temporary fix.

I laughed and finished my pie. "Someday. Not sure though, maybe."

"'Maybe?' Hmph," she scoffed then sighed. "I see you still haven't learned how to leave those fast ass girls alone."

My smile faded and I didn't respond. She smirked.

"I keep telling you, I know my son. Don't mess this up. Alex is a real good woman. She takes care of your home and your children. You may not be in love with her now, but you will someday. But don't wait for that day to come and pass you by. Alex isn't a stupid girl. And she'll catch you in one of your lies someday."

Thoughts of Tiffany ran around in my head. If I had been still single, I could have seen myself dating her, well at least for a little while. There was something intriguing, fascinating, about her.

"Ma," I began with a sigh. "Of course there is nothing wrong with Alexandria. But, we were brought together by... circumstance. Should I sell myself short because of that?"

She shook her head and waved off my explanation. "Hmph, you know there are days where you remind me so much of your father."

My arms tightened at my sides and I swallowed back a curse that hung on my lips. If she had been a man, I would have hit her.

How the fuck could she compare me to that asshole?

"He was the same way like you," she said, while wiping off the counter. "Always looking for the next best thing. Always waiting for something. Never… satisfied. Couldn't see a good thing right in front of him. Your daddy thought all of you were just 'circumstances' too."

Her words burned a fire in my stomach.

"I am nothing like my father," I corrected, trying not to be disrespectful. She shrugged. Either she didn't notice my attitude change or refuse to acknowledge it.

"You're not. That's why I know you'll do the right thing," she said with a grin. "By the way, how's Rachel? You spoke to her lately? Is she doing well?"

I suppressed a chuckle as I thought of Rachel swinging on the pole. "She's hanging in there."

Ma cast a disapproving glance. "Don't be like that, Braxton. Rachel's a good girl. It's a shame ya'll couldn't work out your issues."

At first, I was comfortable with Rachel and Ma having a relationship while we dated, especially if our relationship was to last. But now that it was over and she kept coming up in conversation, it was just an annoyance—a constant reminder of a girl I was trying to leave in the past. She refused to be forgotten.

"But I'm with Alexandria now, Ma," I reminded her.

She sniffed the air as if I didn't say anything. Her breathing was shallow, almost forced.

"Ma, what's wrong?"

She frowned and shook her head. "Nothing, baby, why you ask?"

I tried to find a delicate way to probe without damaging her pride. "Well, you just look a little tired, that's all. When's the last time you've been to the doctor?"

Her eyes narrowed before her face lit up. "Oh. So that's what's going on, huh? You've been talking to Paris. Was wondering what brought you all the way up here."

Guess it's time to cut the bullshit and get down to business.

"Ma, when's the last time you've been to the doctor?"

"That's none of your business," she snapped, fidgeting with her apron.

"You know I'll find out," I said with a shrug. "Why are you being so secretive? Why did I have to hear from Paris that you weren't feeling well, when I talk to you every day?"

"I feel fine."

"You've lost weight."

She opened her mouth to argue but thought against it. With a heavy sigh, she conceded and sat beside me. "Three weeks ago, I went to the clinic," she started, avoiding eye contact. "It's just my heart is not working the way it use to. No big deal. It's what happens when you get to be my age."

I jumped out my chair before I knew what I was doing. "Your heart! Ma, why didn't you tell me? I could've had the best doctors see for themselves. Heart disease is serious, you can't take this lightly!"

How could she not tell me about this? My mind raced with images of heart attacks, hospitals, surgeries, operating rooms, and death.

Damn, not Ma!

"'Cause I don't want to focus on it, Braxton! And I'm fine. I'm a grown woman and I can take care of myself. I just wish your nosy sister would mind her business!"

She stared off, a flicker a shame crossing her face. Pride is a motherfucker. I sighed and sat back down.

"I'm sorry, Ma. I wasn't thinking. Of course you can take care of yourself, and you have every right to privacy. But I want to help. So can we please make an appointment with a specialist? Please?"

She nodded as she wiped off the table with her hand. "It's probably nothing. Probably just stress," she said then smiled. "But your brother's home now. I won't have nothing to worry about. He'll take care of me."

Yeah right, just like the last time.

Like a telepath, she read my mind and held my hand. "It wasn't his fault Braxton. He wasn't even here."

I leaned back in my chair to make sure Brian wasn't eavesdropping.

"And how long does he plan on staying here?" I whispered.

She shrugged. "Till he gets on his feet, I suppose."

I rolled my eyes and tried to snatch my hand back but she refused to let go.

"Braxton, he's your brother. And family stick together. Remember that."

That was pretty hard to forget.

***

Sleeping in my childhood bed was as comfortable as sleeping on a pile of sharp rocks. The twin mattress was lumpy and sunken. It creaked at the tiniest shift in movement. I slept in my long johns since Ma liked to keep the house just above freezing, with claims of conserving energy at night. The walls of my cramped room were still painted a deep hunter green and the heavy maroon drapes still blocked out the rising sun. On the opposite side of the room was an identical twin bed, with Brian snoring on it.

Ma was up. I could smell biscuits baking in the oven and the bacon sizzling in her cast iron skillet. It had to be at least seven o'clock. Alexandria was probably up, too: feeding the babies breakfast at the custom table with four highchairs that I had made especially for the kids. I missed playing with them. Maybe I should have gone home first. This was a long time to be away from them. Will they even remember me when I get back?

"You up, B?"

I turned and Brian was sitting up in bed, rolling a blunt in his lap.

Figures.

There were a lot of habits I had given up for the sake of my future and weed was one of them. I figured, if I was going to be successful, and not wind up back in Boston, I had to do the opposite of what everyone else was doing back home. Or better yet, do the opposite of what Brian did. If he walked left, I would walk right.

He licked closed his Dutch and smiled. "You wanna take a ride?"

We quickly showered and dressed, sitting at the table for breakfast: grits, eggs, bacon, and fresh biscuits. Ma watched us scarf down our food with a grin, giving Brian an extra spoonful of grits. She was in heaven feeding her boys again, but she looked exhausted. I made a mental note to call a doctor the moment I was out of the house.

Brian asked for the keys to the car and we were off to the one place I knew he would want to visit first: Vin's barber shop. The cowbell on the door rung as we walked in the black-owned shop, wallpapered with yellowing newspaper clippings dating back to the seventies. Vin, sitting in the first chair, lit up as we entered.

"Oh my goodness! Well look who it is, the Earwood Boys!"

Brain skipped straight for Vin's chair and hugged him. Man, it felt good to hear our old nickname. Everyone in the neighborhood knew us as the Earwood Boys, the two polar opposite brothers who did almost everything together. It was a little comforting being surrounded by the people who truly knew me. Most of the time, it felt as if no one knew the real Braxton Earwood.

Not even my wife.

"Welcome back, Brian! I heard you were getting out this week! Damn boy, look at all that hair," Vin said, as he inspected the long braids Nina had redone last night.

"Thanks, Vin! It feels good to be back," Brian said.

"How long was you away? A year?"

"Five long years! Ain't nothing, tho."

I greeted the shop staples, sitting in the same seats that they sat in when I first started going to Vin's as a kid. Vin was known for the sharpest cuts. Dudes waited hours just to sit in his chair.

"And look who else come around to grace us with his presence. Good to see you, Braxton!"

"Likewise, old man," I said, giving him a hug. "You're still my favorite barber."

He gives me a hard pat on the back, holding my arms, staring proudly.

"Hey, how all them babies? You know, I got your picture up on my wall over there." He pointed over to a framed newspaper clipping of Alexandria, the kids, and myself hanging in the corner.

"I tell everyone that comes in here, I used to cut that boys hair!"

I chuckled at the picture: Alexandria and I bookending four car seats, sitting on a hospital bed. The publicist from the hospital begged us for one photo to keep the press from hounding the staff. Alexandria was still recovering from her surgery, and regrets to this day that she didn't take a moment to straighten her hair or do her makeup.

"I look homeless," she had cried, when the photos hit the papers. "How could you let them take that picture? You know I was high on everything, I wasn't thinking with all cylinders working!"

Brian glanced at the picture with zero interest, appearing unimpressed. He hadn't asked about the kids, and I'm sure if it wasn't for my Ma's bragging, he probably wouldn't even know I had any.

"Hey yo, Vin, I need you to handle this right quick," Brian laughed, messing with his hair.

"Of course! Sit yourself right on down here."

Brian jumped into the chair as Vin draped a smock around him while I sat in the small waiting area.

"So, what'll it be?" Vin asked, cleaning his clippers while examining Brian's hair.

"Just a shape up. We can't all be pretty boys like B over there."

Vin chuckled and I remained silent. That was only the start of Brian's snarky jokes and digs. Acknowledging them would only make it worse.

"So what's been going on man, how's life?" Vin asked. I wasn't sure who he was speaking to at first until he glanced up at me. The clippers clicked on, creating a low buzz throughout the small shop.

"Life's been good man, just in town checking on Ma."

"Oh yeah. And how she's doing?" Vin asked, peering over his glasses. It was well-known he'd had a crush on Ma ever since Pops left, but was too scared of us to act on it. Brian raised an eyebrow and tensed.

"She's good," Brian said in a clipped tone.

"She's aight, Vin," I said, laughing at Brian's overprotective nature. Ma was a grown woman, she could do what she wanted to, and Vin was a good man. I wouldn't be mad if they started dating. But Brian, he was still holding on to hope that Pops was going to come home, for good.

Vin cleared his throat. "Well, I'm just waiting for the invitation to your wedding. I'm sure it got lost in the mail somewhere. 'Cause that's a good woman having all those kids for you."

I straightened in my chair, avoiding eye contact.

"She's ok. We'll see," I said flatly.

Brian eyed me with a smirk.

"And you, Brian," Vin says, trying to divert the attention from me. "What will you be up to now that you're a free man?"

Brian shrugged, trying not to move too much so Vin wouldn't nick him.

"I don't know. Just need to get back on my feet, you know. Sounds crazy, but I was running shit up in there. Had a system for everything. Mad stressful, so I was thinking I just need to take a break, you know. Maybe hang out for a while."

His eyes darted towards me then quickly glanced away.

Hang out? Oh hell no.

"Hang out," I repeated, trying to keep my voice even but my sarcasm came seeping through. "So how long you plan on 'hanging out' at Ma's?"

Brian arched his eyebrow then chuckled.

"I was wondering when you were gonna ask me that."

My Blackberry buzzed. New text message from Tiffany.

I don't know why, but I kinda miss your face.

I smiled, thinking of her sweet smile. It was cool how she didn't trip about cancelling plans. Unlike Alexandria, Tiffany wasn't a nag. I would have loved to have that sort of peace in my life on a daily basis.

"Uh-oh," Brian said with a chuckle. "I don't think your *wife* is putting that smile on your face."

Vin's head snapped up. "Wait, you're married already? Well, congratulations!"

Fuck, now the whole 'hood will know!

"You still haven't answered my question, Brian," I snapped, pretending not to hear Vin.

"What business is it of yours? That's between me and Ma. Ain't none of your business."

My patience was growing thin. "I'm just wondering how much money you gonna drain Ma for this time, or if you gonna get the house shot up again."

The shop grew quiet. Brian glared over at me while Vin pretended to concentrate on the back of Brian's head.

I hope he fucks up his line or at least nicks him good.

"Oh I see, you're just here to judge me, right? You come up all this way just to put my shit on blast. I don't how many times I got to tell you, that shit wasn't my fault. But you can be easy, I ain't taking Ma's money. Even if she offers it. I'ma get a job."

I chuckled. "Yeah, that's what you said last time."

Brian's eyes narrowed as he measured me. "Or, maybe I'll go down to Atlanta, help my new sister-in-law take care of my nieces and nephews. I'm sure she'll *love* my company. Bet I'll treat her better than you're whack ass ever had."

I knew he was just talking shit, but the idea of him even touching Alexandria made me want to drag him outside and smash his head into the nearest car window. Alexandria was mine and I'd fucking kill Brian if he ever came near her. Brian smirked, which only made my blood boil, and my practiced composure was starting to fade quick. Nothing could calm me down now. Just as I was about to stand up and attack, Vin jumped in with some news.

"I saw y'all Daddy the other day."

Both of our eyes lit up but we remained still.

"Where?" Brian asked, trying to reel back his apparent eagerness. He was always searching for the man I gave up on years ago.

"Came to Ms. Jones birthday party few weeks back. Same Jimmy. Ain't changed one bit."

"He... he still around?" Brian asked, turning to face Vin. "Do you know where he is? Did he say where he's staying?"

I groaned, tired of seeing Brian look so pathetic with his daddy issues.

"Damn, would you give it a rest," I said. "Why you still asking about him? He never asks about us. He doesn't want anything to do with us."

Brian rolled his eyes and waved me off with a middle finger.

"Well, you know how he do," Vin said, cautiously. "Breezes through every few weeks or so. Hit up his old spots, see some folks, comes by to get a line up, then poof!"

Wonder if he has stopped by Ma's? Would she have told me?

Pops resurfaced from time to time while I was growing up. Only to stop by, pretend he cared, and take whatever money we had before disappearing again. During undergrad, he actually showed up on my campus and claimed I owed him for my success. I made it clear that if he ever came within a foot of me again I'd shove a gun in his mouth.

"So, if I give you my number, you think you can give it to him the next time you see him?" Brian asked, nervously. "I can write it down, all you need to do it give it to him."

Unbelievable.

"You know that asshole is not gonna call you, right? Unless he needs money, which you don't have to give."

He jumped up and I was on my feet before he crossed the room.

"Hey! Y'all cut that out," Vin yelled but stayed back. "Y'all brothers! You shouldn't be fighting like this."

Brian stood inches from my face, huffing like a bull. I was just waiting for him to make the first move.

"I know it was you who told Pops not to come around us no more. You threatened him and told him to stay away from us. You ain't had the right to make that type of decision for us! That was fucked up, B!"

"I told him to stay away from me and Ma. I didn't say nothing about you. He made that decision long ago. Back when you were first born."

Brian's eyes widened for a brief second then narrowed. I hit several nerves, but he needed to know the truth. Everyone in the shop waited for his hot-headed reaction, the Brian we all knew well. Instead, he exhaled and smirked.

"You know what your problem is," he said in a low voice. "You just like him. As much you try running from him, doing the opposite of everything he do, you JUST like him. Even the way you treat your girl. You sitting here, acting like you don't want her when you know you do. You probably wanted her even BEFORE all them babies. Just like Pops wanted Ma. He knows it and you know it. He just couldn't get out his own way to admit it. And neither can you."

My jaw tensed. Brian didn't lay one hand on me but his words were strong jabs to the jaw.

"And you know why I didn't follow those dumb ass 'rules' Regal was stuffing in your brain?" Brian chuckled, dropping a few dollars on Vin's chair and throwing his coat back on. "It's because those rules were made for someone going to war. And I ain't going to war with my family, with the people I love, with the people who love me. So, nah, B, you ain't gotta like Pops. But he's family. And no matter what, I don't turn my back on my family. Can't say the same about you."

Brian headed for the door, leaving me speechless.

"Keep following those rules, and one day you gonna wake up and see the trail of bodies you stepped on to get where you are today." He shook his head and let the cowbell clang as he left.

CHAPTER 7

I've never been a fan of long plane rides. They allowed too much time to think and my head was already filled to capacity. When I wasn't thinking about Alexandria and the kids, I was thinking about Ma and her heart condition, or signing the deal with Clint, or Tiffany, or the house for sale, or work, or Brian being back home, or Pops. And if that wasn't enough, the shit Brian said was haunting me. Even though every other word Brian spits is typically a lie, he did spit some truth in Vin's shop.

And the truth: I did want Alexandria before she got pregnant. I never wanted her to move to New York. I wanted her to stay… with me.

But I couldn't just *say* that. You can't just tell a woman you want them. It's a sign of weakness. What kind of punk would I have looked like, giving her the upper hand? Plus, we had… complications.

That last night we spent together in D.C., I planned to fuck the shit out of her, leave her body sore so that she'd remember what she was leaving behind. Instead, I was the one with her body on my brain. The smell of her on my clothes, in my car, on my sheets, was driving me crazy. Even when I moved to Atlanta, I couldn't stop thinking about her. Call her? No way, what kind of punk would I have looked like? Other women were blowing up my phone, why should I have been worried about one chick?

Pride is a motherfucker.

That is why the first time she texted me—a whole month later—I made her wait. The same way she had made me wait. I could play the game just as good as she could. But shit hit the fan when she said she was pregnant. Told me over text, the most passive aggressive, idiotic way to share that type of news. I could have strangled her, but instead I called, said some fucked up shit and she hung up. On ME! It took a week to calm down from that.

When I finally came to my senses, after hours spent in the gym hitting everything in sight, I had a breakthrough—a baby wasn't ideal, but it would bring Alexandria back to me. She'd HAVE to call, she'd HAVE to deal with me, whether she wanted to or not. I wanted her to be mine, unequivocally.

But that all changed the moment she walked into my hotel room. One whiff of her scent was like coke and I was feigning, ready to rip her clothes off. Trying to play it cool, I had slipped into the bathroom just to compose myself. Her effect on me was dangerous.

Shit man, get a hold of yourself.

The door slammed and my heart sped up. I stuck my head back out, worried she'd left, but ready to chase her to the end of the fucking earth if I had to. She was still standing by the door, with some random paper bag by her feet. Her face was pale, her eyes wide—almost frighten, and her stomach, it was much bigger than I was expecting.

Damn, how far along is she? Why the fuck didn't she tell me?

"What the fuck are you doing?" I asked, annoyed that she had waited so long to say something. Did she really think she could do this by herself?

"Well, it's nice to see you too," she snapped, rolling her eyes. "Thanks for the warm welcome."

We were already off to a rocky start. And my dick had gotten harder just looking at her. I slipped back in the bathroom. Only two options presented themselves: fuck her or jerk off. It would take some convincing to pop her clothes off and I needed to get rid of my situation ASAP. I couldn't have her knowing she had such an effect on me. So I beat it and came in a hotel towel, thinking of her right outside my door the entire time.

After I had my faculties back, I joined her in the bedroom, still confused by her appearance. She didn't look healthy. Pregnant women were supposed to have a glow, but that day she looked seasick. What kind of jerk did she take me for? Had she really thought I wouldn't handle my responsibilities as a man? Of course I would help and taken care of her. She didn't have to go through it alone to prove a point. So I told her I wanted to be a part of the child's life and was fully prepare to work something out. And she laughed at me. Laughed! My hands balled into fist.

A punishment fuck would shut that ass up right now.

But before I could throw her on the bed, she dropped the bomb on me: Quadruplets. And I did what any other man would have done, I freaked the fuck out.

WHAT THE FUCK? HOW THE FUCK? WHO THE FUCK?

The dialog went south and she started to walk out. My legs were up, running after her before I could think of what I was doing. She couldn't leave me. Not again. I jumped in front her and slammed the door shut. I was so close I could sniff her hair. Smelled like that sweet oil she liked using to make her hair shiny. Her bottom lip, all thick and juicy, waiting for my kiss, began to tremble before she started to cry.

Shit, not tears. Anything but tears.

I'll admit I'm not the most sensitive dude, but I hate, HATE hurting anyone, especially her. My hands loosened, aching to pull her into my chest. I had wanted to touch her the moment she stepped in my room. But would she let me or would she just push me away? Couldn't have taken that chance, that rejection, so instead, I shoved my hands in my pockets.

"I lost my job today," she mumbled, not able to meet my eyes.

I'll kill those motherfuckers.

I swallowed, imagining running into her office and beating the shit out of whoever fired her. Thinking, *this is what happens when I let her out of my sight. She gets hurt.* But then my co-worker came knocking on the door. I had completely forgotten about our client dinner. Buying myself some time, I left Alexandria in my room, went to dinner, had at least a bottle's worth of Henny, and took a long walk back to my hotel, analyzing all the possible scenarios.

#7 Think three steps ahead in all situations. Take all contingences into account.

If I let her stay in New York with my kids, when would I see them? And how often? How could I control any of the stupid decisions Alexandria tended to make from Atlanta? And who would take care of her? Every question led to the same answer—I needed to be around. In fact, I wanted to be around. But the only way to do that was to bring sand to the beach: moving Alexandria to Atlanta. Making the decision to take time off work was easy. I didn't want to hire a team of nannies and leave it up to Alexandria to care for my kids. I wanted to be the major influence in their life. I wanted to be around so they would know, without question, who their father was.

And right there, the idea solidified. She had to come to Atlanta with me, where I could watch her, keep her from getting hurt. It was logical, she had no other options, and I wasn't taking no for an answer.

But, was Brian right? Had following my rules left people hurt in the process? Was I hurting Alexandria and didn't even know it? I thought being this way, keeping a calm and steady head, helped everyone in the long run. I was able to provide for Ma, for Alexandria, and for the kids. I would have never been able to do all that if I had let feelings cloud my judgment.

But my feelings were all over the place when it came to Alexandria.

***

My flight arrived in Atlanta close to midnight. By the time I reached home, I figured everyone would be asleep. But Bob Marley greeted my ears at the door before Sasha trotted out of the kitchen and found me in the foyer. She did her usual sniffing inspection before letting me pass. I placed my bags by the stairs and followed the music to the kitchen. Alexandria sat at the nook, wearing a long white t-shirt that stopped at her thighs, her hair in a disheveled bun, concentrating on some project spread out on the table, while her foot slowly rocked a cradle next to her.

"Hey, welcome back," she said, her back still facing me. "How was your flight?"

For some reason, hearing her voice put me at ease after my long trip. All I wanted to do was hold her, sniff her neck, stuff myself between her legs, fuck her in a hot shower, and never leave the house again. Until I came within a foot of the table.

"What are you doing?"

She jumped, eyes wide and startled. In her hands, a stack of store coupons and a pair of bright orange scissors.

"What? What's wrong?"

"Why in the hell are you cutting coupons?" I asked, disgusted.

She frowned. "What you mean, WHY? Why not?" She waved me off as if I was the one being ridiculous and returned to her thrifty task, carefully cutting along the lines while continuing to rock the cradle, Lil' Alex asleep inside. The whole scene was eerie, like déjà vu or something. Reminded me of Ma, cutting coupons, stressed out over our food stamps running out, while caring for my infant sister, all after working ten-hour days at the hospital. I hated seeing Ma so beaten and broken. I hated not knowing if we would have enough to eat and swore we would never live through that again.

So why the fuck is my wife cutting coupons for Vienna sausages?

Alexandria had never cut a coupon a day in her life. She couldn't even go to the supermarket without spending less than a hundred dollars. But the idea of her fingers smudging on newspaper clippings, while my son lay sleeping next to her... the idea of my son going through what I did, overwhelmed me. Unable to control myself, I snatched the scissors out of her hands.

"Hey! What the hell?"

She tried to grab them back and I slammed them on the table.

Oh no!

We both froze and glanced in the crib, Lil' Alex continued to sleep through the noise.

"Are you crazy?" Alexandria asked under her breath with a scowl, her arms crossed.

"Why are you doing this?" I asked, as I sat next to her, pushing the coupons out of my sight.

She shrugged. "Well, I figured since we're short on cash, I might as well help out anyway I can."

"What makes you assume we're 'short on cash'?"

"Well, that's why you married me isn't it," she said, throwing our quickie wedding in my face.

I sighed. "Alexandria, we're not bankrupt."

She bit her lower lip and looked away. "I know that. I just figured…"

"No more coupons. We don't need them."

"Braxton, they're just coupons. I didn't think I'd save the house from foreclosure by saving forty cents on Hamburger Helper. But we do have four children, and last time I checked, kids ain't cheap. We should start conserving some. Or maybe just save up for other things."

She shrugged, idly rubbing her finger.

Oh… her finger!

I smirked and relaxed, unbuttoning my collar. "Other things, like a ring, perhaps?"

She shrugged again and tried to hide a grin. "Maybe."

No matter how she tries to beat around the bush, I could still read her like a Dr. Seuss book. A ring must be the equivalent to a Super Bowl trophy for her to go through all this trouble. She didn't even like Hamburger Helper.

A ring had little significance to anyone in this day and age. A ring won't stop a woman from flirting with a man at a bar, nor does it stop a man from sleeping with someone else's wife. A ring could just as easily be taken off.

I should know.

I didn't need nor want a ring. But it would be hard convincing Alexandria of the same mindset.

But perhaps with a few distractions…

Her t-shirt was just short enough to expose her thighs and hot pink panties. It took my dick three seconds to get hard. I slipped my arms around her waist and lifted her onto the table. She gasped a bit but didn't fight me as I ripped off her shirt and crashed into her lips. Our tongues mashed together. She kissed back fiercely. All the fight left me, every ounce of stress melted. That was what made her so addictive, the way she made everything disappear.

She smiled as she unbuckled my belt and I climbed on top of her, my pants hanging around my ankles. I entered her slow, but the way we both craved each other, slow wasn't going to quench our need this time. I grabbed the edge of the table as it creaked louder than her pants.

"You're gonna break the table," she gasped with a moan.

"I don't care."

But then we heard one of the kids crying in the distance.

Shit.

Alexandria's face tensed up as the cries grew louder. She grasped my shoulders, glancing at the baby monitor.

"It's ok, baby... Mommy's coming!"

I stroked harder and she suppressed a scream. More cries—the kids were a distraction, I couldn't concentrate.

"Okay, you gotta let me up," Alexandria gasped, attempting to push away, but I wouldn't move.

In a minute, just let me nut first.

I tangled my fingers in her hair, thrusting into her like a wild man.

"Braxton, they're crying," she whimpered.

You don't think I know that?

I couldn't just stop in the middle of what I was doing. Or who I was doing. "They're alright, just give me a second."

She pushed at my chest this time. "A second? No, get up!"

I tried to keep my place, my momentum, but between Alexandria's unwillingness and the kids screaming, I lost focus and my dick went limp. Alexandria pushed me and wiggled off the table. The sexual frustration exploded from my lips.

"Fuck, Alexandria!"

"What?" she asked, winded as she threw her shirt back on. Lil' Alex started to stir, the noises disturbing his slumber.

"What you mean, 'What?' You know what!"

She shrugged. "What do you want me to do, the kids are crying!"

"But we haven't had sex in over a week."

As soon as I said the words I regretted it. Alexandria turned around slow, hands locked on her hip.

"Oh really? And who's fault is that?" she snapped, her neck rolling.

I remained silent, pulling up my pants, hoping it would just blow over.

"Never mind, forget it. Go check on the kids," I ordered.

"No, really, Braxton, I wanna know. Because last time I checked, the furthest I've been is to the fucking mailbox. So please, enlighten me. Why haven't we had sex it over a week?"

The screams in the nursery blared through the monitor. Alexandria ignored them, willing to let the babies cry just to prove a point. I stormed passed her towards the nursery.

The kids believed there was no 'I' in team, thus, if one was awake, they were all awake, screaming from their cribs like an off key symphony. I lifted Brandi and Aiden out and rubbed their backs, attempting to sooth their nerves.

We took too long to check on them. They probably thought we'd abandon them.

Alexandria stormed in, cradling a few bottles while balancing Lil' Alex. Beth stood in her crib reaching her small little hands out to her. Face soaked with tears, lips trembling.

"Aren't you gonna get Beth?"

"I only have two hands, Braxton! Must I keep on reminding you?" she snapped and turned towards Beth. "It's okay, Bethy baby. Mommy's here."

She leaned down and kissed her head. Beth jumped up and down, screaming louder, demanding to be held.

I balanced Brandi and Aiden in one arm and scooped up Beth with the other. Her little hands pushed at my chest. She didn't want me, she wanted her mother.

"I can't believe you'd complain about not getting enough sex," she barked over the kid's cries.

"Well you always start snoring around eight thirty! What do you expect?"

"I'm sleep at eight thirty because I'm chasing your children around all day. And you've been gone for over a week!"

"Fine. Whatever!"

Damn, she could beat a dead horse to dust. I'm not even home an hour and she's on my ass.

She stormed over and grabbed Bethany out my hands. I sat on the daybed, bouncing the kids in my arms, trying to comfort them.

She scoffed. "You're such a fucking jerk," she whispered as she sat down in the rocking chair across the room. The kids were simmering down in her lap.

"Oh yeah, because you're such a delight to deal with every day."

***

"Oh my gosh! You guys are so cute!"

Kennedy sat in the middle of my living room, bouncing Brandi on her lap and it took all of my efforts to keep myself from grabbing her away. Besides Kennedy, three of Alexandria's other girlfriends were playing with the rest of the children. They were in town for a wedding and came to visit the kids before taking Alexandria for a girl's night out. Alexandria had been anticipating their arrival for at least three months. She went to Lenox mall on at least four separate occasions, looking for the perfect outfit.

"I haven't had one childless or man-less night in over a year!"

Besides us, Alexandria didn't have anyone in Atlanta and was so focused on the kids that she rarely left the house. It meant everything to her just to have one night to be herself. As much as I didn't want to admit it, she deserved it. I agreed to babysit the kids to let her have her fun and she reminded me every week so I wouldn't forget.

By the time her friends had arrived, Alexandria had the kids fed, bathed, and in their pajamas, ready for bed. As she beautified, I stood by the stairs and watched the kids play with their new company, waiting for one of them to fuck up so I could kick them out of my house. Especially Kennedy.

"So where y'all going tonight?" I asked.

"The Velvet Room," Kennedy said, leaving lipstick stains on Brandi's cheek. "She says you always go there and wanted to check it out."

Good, a place I know. I'll call Trey to keep an eye on her.

Alexandria was more than capable of handling herself, but my chest tightened at the thought of her being anywhere without me. Ever since I met her, I'd came down with this weird possessive disease that made me want to keep her within arm's reach at all times. I fucking hated being *that* guy.

"If you want, I can make a call and put you ladies on the VIP list," I offered.

Her friends, surprised by the hospitality nodded. All thankful, except for Kennedy.

"Nah, we good. We're already on a list." The group scowled at her.

"I bet you are," I chuckled, her snarky attitude pure comedy.

Alexandria emerged from the bedroom, dressed in a pair of tight, dark blue jeans, a purple ruffled top and black heels. Hair all curly, wearing new makeup with some of that glossy stuff that made her lips look edible. I couldn't stop staring; I wanted to drag her back upstairs and rip those jeans down.

Wow.

At first she came down the stairs skipping, smile beaming, but then hesitated on the first landing, her face going blank. She measured each of her friends' outfits, all scandalous compared to her modest attire.

"Hey girl, you ready?" Kennedy asked, oblivious of Alexandria's demeanor. Or perhaps I was the only one paying attention. Whatever confidence she had before she walked downstairs had evaporated.

"Ummm… in a minute," she mumbled. "I… uhhh… think I forgot something." She doubled back and I rushed after her, catching her on the first landing.

"Where do you think you are going?" I asked, holding her by the arm.

"I'm just going to go change," she whispered, shying away from my stare.

"What for?"

She glanced over at her friends, each pretending they weren't listening to our conversation.

"I…I don't know. I just feel…a little underdressed. That's all," she said sheepishly. "It's silly. I just haven't gone out in a while."

After months of talking about this one night, Alexandria looked miserable. I hated that she thought she was less than worthy of attention because she wasn't dressed like a groupie. She was stunning, but if I told her that, she wouldn't believe me. So I told her something she would believe I would say.

"Alexandria, you're being ridiculous. You look fine."

"I look like somebody's Momma," she said, rolling her eyes.

"You *are* somebody's Momma. And somebody's wife. You don't need to dress like some ho' to have a good time." I said that last part a little louder, directing it more towards Kennedy, who was wearing a tight leopard dress with half her double-D cleavage hanging out.

"I don't know," she mumbled, playing with the end of her top, her eyes plastered to the floor.

Nothing irritated me more than convincing this woman—whose arresting beauty far surpassed her friends—that she was gorgeous enough to go out in a sea of tasteless smuts wearing just jeans and a shirt. The only person that's allowed to make her question her sanity is me.

I sighed and took a step further into her personal space, pinning her to the wall. She gazed up at me, at first confused then captivated, as I wrapped my arms around her waist, smiling.

"Alexandria, you look fine," I whispered, lips grazing her ear. "Go, have a good time. And when you get home, I'll be waiting. Maybe in those red boxers you love so much."

Her skin grew hotter under my touch and she nodded, wordless. The anticipation of sex was enough to distract her, stroke her ego and give her the much-needed boost of confidence. I unlocked myself from around her waist and dragged her back down the stairs.

"Make sure she has a good time," I ordered Kennedy and she rolled her eyes at me.

Alexandria walked a bit taller as she kissed the kids goodbye. Lil' Alex fussed, sensing his mother leaving. I picked him up out of the playpen, but to no avail. Alexandria's friends gushed one more time before sitting the babies down and heading out the door. It took Alexandria another ten minutes to tear herself away.

"I love you guys. See you soon. Mommy will be back real soon!"

Grinning, she mouthed a 'thanks' and ran out the door. And that tightness in my chest squeezed a little harder. I sent Trey her picture with a text:

Anything happens to this woman, I'll burn the place down with everyone inside.

Lil' Alex smacked my phone screen and grins. "Subtle, right?"

***

The kids, exhausted by all the unexpected fun, made it a quarter of the way through a Disney movie before falling asleep on top of me. One by one, I carried them upstairs and tucked them into their cribs. Around ten o'clock, while watching a little ESPN, a message popped up from Tiffany:

Hey boo! What's up?

Hmmmm... it would be rude to ignore her. Again.

With no Alexandria around to monitor my every move, I leaned back in my recliner and dialed her number.

"Well hello! This is a surprise! You're actually calling me," she squeaked.

"Knock it off, I call you," I said with a smirk. Glasses clinked and music blasted behind her.

"Yeah sure, whatever," she giggled.

"So what's up? Sounds like you're busy."

"Oh, it's nothing," she said right before a door slammed and I hear a toilet flush. "What are you up to?"

"Just watching TV."

"On a Saturday night? You're not going out?"

"Nah. I'm a grown ass man. I don't need to go out every night."

"You don't have a date?"

"Nope." Technically, that wasn't a lie. I didn't have a date. Alexandria was out partying.

"Oh! Sooooo… when are you coming back to D.C.?"

"When are you coming to ATL?"

"Whenever you invite me," she purred.

I smiled, knowing that would never happen.

***

The screaming woke me up. Half-asleep, I checked the baby monitor. Silence, but I still heard screams, far off and muffled. They weren't screams of pain, more like screams of joy, like college kids on spring break. I hopped out of bed and peered out the window. Alexandria was lying in the grass, face down.

My feet barely touched the stairs as I flew out the door. "ALEX!"

Her head popped up, a goofy smile painted across her lips.

"Heyyyyy, baby!" she said, slurring her words as she stumbled to find her legs, trying to lift herself up.

"What the fuck?"

"HONEY!!! I'm home," she said, followed by a cackle.

I bound towards her as the neighbor's porch light came on.

Shit.

"Keep your voice down," I chastised. "You want to wake the whole neighborhood?"

A fit of giggles slipped through her muffled mouth and she fell to the ground again. Kennedy stood by her side cracking up, trying to help her onto her feet. I slapped her hands away and lifted Alexandria up, checking her pupils. She couldn't just be drunk; she seemed drugged.

"What's wrong with her?" I barked.

"Nothing!" Kennedy laughed, wobbling in her heels. "Alex had just a little too much to drink."

"Define a little?"

"Pezzztron babe! Loosey for the Goosey!" Alexandria sang, her arms flinging around.

"You gave her tequila AND vodka?"

"Not my fault," Kennedy said with a sly grin. "Your boy showed us a good time. And you know she can't hold her liquor."

Kennedy did this on purpose, the stupid bitch!

Alexandria looked over at her friends still sitting in the car.

"Girls, girls! This is my huzzzzband! Isn't he cute?" She fell into my arms and I almost lost it.

I let her out of my sight for one night and look what happens. Fuck!

I scooped her up and glared at Kennedy.

"I'm taking her inside. You can go now," I said, heading for the door without giving Kennedy a chance to respond. Alexandria pulled herself up in my arms and shouted over my shoulder.

"Goodnight girls! I'm about to get me some dick tonight!"

Her friends roared with laughter.

"Alexandria, shut up! You'll wake the babies," I ordered as I carried her inside, shutting the door.

"Babies? Oh right, right babies! Did you know I have four of them?"

"Yes, I know. I have four too."

I placed her on the sofa and she rolled on the floor with a thud.

Fuck, I haven't had to take care of a drunken fool since college.

Alexandria's struggle to stand up was comical: butt in the air, hands on the floor as she coached herself through her own movements. I poked her with one finger and she tumbled back down as if I had thrown her. She stared up at me, smiling with an insane goofy grin.

"Hmmm…you're cute," she chirped.

"No way," I said, shaking my head. "You can't go upstairs like this. You'll wake up the kids."

"But I'm so sleeeeeepy! I wanna lay down," she begged.

"We'll lay down here."

"No!"

"Shhhh!"

She slapped her hands together in prayer. "Pleezzzzzz! I'll be good! I promise!"

She gave me the big puppy-dog eyes while pleading, and against my better judgment, I relented.

"Aight, fine," I groaned. I lifted her up over my shoulder effortlessly and walked upstairs. She squirmed and wiggled in my arms.

"Ohhh… you're tickling me. Stop!"

"Be quiet," I scolded in a hush whisper.

"Wow, you have a nice butt," she said and gave my ass a slap.

I dropped her on the bed and she bounced twice with a giggle.

"Weeeee…that was fun! Let's do it again!"

A cry crackled in the monitor on the nightstand. "Fuck! Now you've done it. And I think it's Alex."

"Oooo! Oooo! I'll do it! Give me a bottle! I'll bring it to him. I'm his mother," she said as she stood, nearly falling. I shoved her back on the bed and passed her a bottle of water instead.

"No! You stay your drunk ass here and drink the rest of this water."

"But I'm not thirsty," she whined.

"Shhhhh…You need to sober up."

She pouted and flopped herself on the bed while I rushed into the nursery, straight to Lil' Alex's crib with a bottle, afraid that he'd cry loud enough to wake the others.

"It's ok, buddy, here you go."

He stopped crying and stared up me. Just sitting up, holding his feet, as if there was nothing wrong with being wide awake in the middle of the night.

Hmmm. You're ok?

"Huh, it's the funniest thing," I said as I closed our bedroom door. "Alex was awake, just chilling in his crib. He didn't even want the bottle and then he…"

On the bed, Alexandria sat up on her knees, staring at me in awe. Almost the same way Lil' Alex had gazed at me.

"What?" I said, looking around me. "What are you looking at?"

She gasped like she had stopped breathing for a moment.

"Wow, it's amazing! I still get butterflies when you walk into a room," she whispered, rubbing her stomach as if trying to settle them. I didn't know what to say so I just stood there.

"I love you soooo much," she said. "Like, you don't even know."

"That's nice, drunky," I chortled.

"No, no, no, I'm serious! I mean it. I am sooo in love with you. I'm sooo happy. I've been in love with you from the very beginning and I think I didn't even know it."

My stomach clinched up, legs wanting to run out the door, away from her and the wall she was about to break down.

What is she doing? This isn't who we are? We don't talk about our feeling!

"Alexandria? I—"

"I know you didn't want children, or me, but isn't this great? Aren't we amazing? Been through fucking hell, made four kids, and I still managed to be in love with you."

If people really show their true selves when they're drunk, then Alexandria was confessing her love for me. A love she has had for a while. Meanwhile, I was completely sober and ready to tell her how much I loved her smell, the way she tastes, or how some days I couldn't imagine life without her, but I couldn't utter a word. So many thoughts flew through my head, including a pinch of guilt. She fell back on the bed and smiled.

"Can we have sex now?" she asked, like a child asking for ice cream. I laughed as I took off my shirt.

"Sure."

She wiggled out of her pants and flung off her top. If I had seen her panties before, she would've never made it out the door. Black sheer with a matching bra—sexy as fuck. She snatched me by the waistband towards her and threw me on the bed. Skipping the foreplay. I welcomed her drunken aggression.

She grinned, kissing down my chest, pulling down my pants. I cupped her tits, rubbing my thumb against the smooth fabric.

"Take this off," I ordered, unhooking her bra and throwing it across the room. She giggled, sitting up to look down at me. Her titties were always the perfect size, but after the babies they were bigger and bouncier than before. I loved sucking on them. I sat up, cupping the back of her head to tongue her down. She moaned, rubbing herself on my dick.

"This too," I whispered against her neck and ripped off her panties. The moment I tore them off, she pushed me back down and jumped on top, bucking against my dick. I stuffed into her and she let out a loud gasp. "Shhhh... keep quiet."

Supporting herself on my chest, she rode my dick with a cocky expression, like she knew how much I needed her, and it drove me crazy to be so powerless. Up and down, pushing hard, faster, I gripped her waist, cupping her ass, which only made her fuck me harder.

God damn she feels good.

I tried to hold back, but her waist was winning the battle. Her eyes started to roll, her muscles pinching around my dick. I reached down and rubbed a thumb on her clit. She gasped and I shot up, locking my mouth on hers, pushing my tongue down her throat to keep her from screaming.

She came hard and fast, the pulsing around my dick went on forever and I couldn't hold it in any longer. I let out a grunt and we dropped on the bed in exhaustion. She curled up on my chest and passed out with a dopey smile. I rubbed the apples of her cheek with a chuckle.

She is such an adorable goofball.

**

"I think we should hook Kevin up with Kennedy," Alexandria said, joining me on the backyard deck. She placed the baby monitor on the table before zipping up her jacket. We were having a small evening barbeque, just the two of us. Grilling is a specialty of mine (Of course, because real men know how to control fire). Besides, I liked cooking for her now and then. I enjoyed feeding her. There is power in food.

"Kevin who?"

"Your cousin Kevin."

I looked up to see if she was joking. She wore an eager grin.

"No. Absolutely not."

The steaks sizzled on the grill as I flipped them over. Her smiled dropped.

"Why not?" Alexandria whined. "They're both in D.C., both single. They would be really cute together."

"Is Kennedy ever really single?" I asked, shaking my head.

"What's that supposed to mean?"

"It means she always has some dude in her back pocket. She's a cheater. Once a cheater, always a cheater."

"What? That's not fair! She's never cheated on anyone."

Ha. She's cheated on you.

"Technically, no she hasn't cheated on someone," I said, grabbing the medium rare T-bones off the grill. "But she has willingly participated in the demise of several relationships. She fucks with dudes that have no problem cheating, fully aware that there is another woman in the picture. She simply has no moral standing when it comes to respecting other people's situations. Can't expect to develop any type of meaningful relationship with that type of woman."

Alexandria's face went blank. She stopped tossing the salad and flopped into a chair like the wind was knocked out of her.

"So what does that say… about me? About us?"

Fuck! Walked right into that shit storm.

She fidgeted with her hands, the hurt evident as her eyes began to water. If she had started to cry, I would have lost my shit.

"Well... we're... different," I said, sitting the steaks in front of her, hoping food would be enough of a distraction. She rolled her eyes, giving me a look as if to say "yeah right."

"Damn, I'm a home wrecker," she mumbled. "They have websites dedicated to harlots like me."

"Don't be ridiculous. There was no home to wreck. Like I said, Rachel and I were done long before you walked into the picture."

"Oh yeah?" she challenged. "Did she know that? Seemed like a pretty one-sided understanding to me."

I sucked in some air, pretending to be annoyed, not willing to concede to her point.

"We weren't married, Alexandria. It's not like I walked out on my family."

"But you *were* very much involved. Then here I come, messing with you, knowing damn well you had a girl at home. Ruining her chance at a perfect life. God! I feel horrible."

She held her head as if it was too heavy to keep up. I hated the way she took all of this on. She felt too deeply. Why couldn't she just focus on herself, rather than worrying about everyone else?

"Have you... talked?" she begged, looking up at me. "Do you know how she's doing? Is she okay?"

"She's hanging in there. I'm sure dancing up a storm since I've been gone," I said, holding back a smirk.

"Braxton, I'm serious! I can't help but to put myself in her shoes. She's probably seen all the papers, knows about you, me, and the kids. I would be devastated if the man I loved just moved on so easily... to do so well... with the girl he cheated on me with. How would I move on from something like that? How could I ever trust another man after that? It would be life-altering. I would probably never be the same."

The familiar burn of guilt smoked up my chest. Could I have driven Rachel off the deep end? Am I responsible for what she has become? Yeah, the way everything went down was fucked up, and can't imagine how it looked from Rachel's perspective. But I refused to be a scapegoat for a grown woman's self-sabotage.

"Look," I said in an even tone. "I'm serious. We are different. Our circumstances from the very beginning were different. We established we were never a one-night stand, we had...well, have, I don't know, this something. And look how we turned out. Hell, look how many kids we have. Quadruplets? People don't even know how to spell that. If that doesn't tell you something about our fate, if that isn't evidence enough to prove we're the exception to the rule, I don't know what would."

Alexandria muddled it over, pouring herself more red wine, and I took a huge sigh of relief, amazed that my quick thinking defused that ticking time bomb. A little alcohol always helps ease tension. *So does sex.*

But the truth: kids aside, we really *were* different. And we had this chemistry. I knew that from the very first moment I saw her, something along the lines of lust at first sight.

I remember that day like it was yesterday. As a last minute favor to my law school professor, I had joined as guest panelist at the Washington Digital Media Conference. There I was, sitting on stage, bored out of my fucking mind, but not eager to leave because then I would have to go back home to deal with Rachel and her non-stop nagging, when I first noticed Alexandria in the audience. It was as if a spotlight had come out of nowhere, shining right over her. She had on this tight cream-colored v-neck dress with some tan boots. Reminded me of a slice of cheesecake, delicious, creamy, moist… I couldn't keep my eyes off her. Her lips were plump and glossy, her hair long and curly, and I wanted nothing more than those perfect fingers with the pretty pink nails wrapped around my dick.

She hadn't notice me staring, too busy taking notes. At one point her pen had run out of ink and she leaned over to grab another one out of her bag, giving me full view of her black lace bra, her thick titties stuffed inside. She sat back up, crossed her legs and stretched her neck, rotating her head with her eyes closed, almost in slow motion. I pulled at my collar, neck steaming, ready to jump off stage and climb over people's heads until I reached her. When her eyes opened, our eyes locked and then… something happened—the heat turned up, lights dimmed, voices faded away, and this pulse, this sonic vibration around the room, hit my dick with enough force to almost knock me out my seat. All I could think was how amazing her nipples would feel in my mouth. How I wanted to grab the thickness of her thighs and palm her ass. How I wanted to fuck the shit out of her. How lightheaded I'd feel after having the best nut in my entire life.

"Braxton? Braxton?"

The current Alexandria stared at me, steak stuck on her fork dripping with A1 sauce.

She rarely curled her hair anymore. Jeans and sneakers were her new best friends.

"What are you doing?" she asked, motioning towards my arms, one hand on my dick, and the other rubbing her crotch, my face damn near in her chest. She chuckled and I straightened up, snatching both hands back and cleared my throat, no longer hungry for steak.

"Nothing," I grinned. "Just making myself comfortable. Hurry up and finish your food so I can have my dessert."

***

"Let's just clean up in the morning," Alexandria sighed with a satisfied smirk, lying on top of me after a marathon of fucking.

"We left the animals a tasty dinner tonight."

She giggled and it was always the sweetest sound. I buried my nose in her hair, inhaling. She still used the Carol's Daughter shampoo I bought her last Christmas, and mixed with her own scent, she smelled like fresh oranges and butter cake. An intoxicating, arousing aroma, I could smell her all day, but I'd never tell her that.

"Did you mean it, what you said back there?" she asked, curled up in the nook of my arm. She fit perfectly, like her body was made just for me to hold, but I'd never tell her that either.

"I said a lot of things. Be more specific."

"About us... and fate," she whispered into my side, kissing my chest. I relished the sensation. Her lips felt too damn good.

"Yeah. I did," I said, gliding a finger up her long back.

She snuggled a little closer. "Me too. I keep thinking back on all those stupid arguments we had. Just seems so trivial now."

I sighed. "We were different people back then."

"Is everything different now?" she asked, reluctantly.

"Elaborate."

"Is... sex, different to you now?"

This was a double-edged sword type of question. One semi-wrong answer could lead to a vibe-killing argument that I wasn't in the mood for.

"It's the same. Actually, better." That wasn't a lie. She was more in tune with her body, and I could make her come before she could scream she's about to.

"But, I'm all fat now," she whined. "My stomach is all flabby. And these stretch marks... I swear those kids used me as an Etch-A-Sketch."

"Really? I didn't even notice." That wasn't a lie. Yes, Alexandria's body had gone through several changes and was a bit thicker in some areas, but it made no difference to me.

"What about… me?"

"Define *me*."

Her face grew red. "Am I still tight… down there, or do you feel like you're fucking the Grand Canyon?"

I laughed, kissing her temple. Her pussy was still tighter than a shrunken leather glove.

Thank God for C-Sections.

"You're ok," I lied and she rolled her eyes.

"Anyways, I think I want to get a tummy tuck. I feel like I have an unused kangaroo pouch."

"Whatever, I think you're fine. So what you're a kangaroo, you're my kangaroo."

She paused for a beat. "Braxton, that was the most romantic thing you've ever said to me," she said and kissed my cheek.

"I have my moments."

She giggled. "Ok, tell me something I don't know about you."

This old game… ha!

I snuggled her closer, resting my chin on her head.

"Let's see… did you know I scored a 1500 on my SATs?"

"Wait a second. That is damn near perfect. That's like… impossible. How?!"

I shrugged. "Photographic memory."

I hadn't known anything about the SATs until the day before the test. My guidance counselor didn't expect me to go to college and neglected to inform me, even though I had the highest GPA of my class. The day after Regal's funeral, I stole a guide from the library, and read it cover to cover. With the help of my photographic memory, I scored high enough to land a full scholarship to Georgetown University, and was the first to attend college in my family.

"Oh shit," she laughed, kissing my chest. "I'm fucking Rain Man."

"Aight, smart ass," I said, tickling her side. "What about you? Tell me something I don't know about you."

"Well, there *is* something I've been meaning to tell you," she said, sheepishly. "But it's kind of embarrassing."

"Let me guess. You used to pee in the bed until high school?"

"No. And, eww! Nothing like that." She exhaled and closed her eyes. "You… were my first."

"First what?"

She slapped both hands over her face and remained quiet. It took a moment before it hit me and I shot up.

"Wait, are you saying I was your first? Like, first, FIRST?! THE first?"

She nodded, refusing to look at me.

Holy shit.

"Alex… I…Why didn't you tell me?"

"I don't know," she exclaimed. "I guess I was embarrassed. It was hard being the twenty-four year old virgin!"

I rubbed my head. "Shit, I don't believe it!"

"You mean you couldn't tell?"

"No! Not at all," I said, mind blown, thinking back to that first time. Yeah, she seemed nervous, but nothing out of the normal, and I was so fucking horny I couldn't see straight. I shook my head. "You should have told me."

"I didn't want you to freak out!"

She had a point. Not easy being a chick's first, especially some chick you were just fuck buddies with. Yet, if I would've known, I may not have been such an animal towards her. Maybe I would've been a bit more… delicate.

"Are you mad?" she asked, biting her lip.

I wanted to be mad, instead this huge grin grew across my face. Call it male ego, but it made me fucking happy as hell that I was the only one who ever had her, and now no one else ever could.

She's alllll mine.

Shockwaves of searing heat spread out in every vein, making my dick swell, and I rolled on top of her, tonguing her down.

"No," I said, breathless. "Not at all."

Pushing the sheets out of my way, I sucked on her nipple, flicking my tongue over it. She moaned, squirming. With her, I had this insatiable appetite and could never get enough. An unquantifiable magnet, a pull that drew me to her, something I'd never experienced before with anyone else.

So why am I fighting it so hard?

Because when it came to Alexandria, nothing was in my control, and the chemistry between us left me irrevocably powerless. And nothing irritated me more than lack of power.

#13 Never let a man or woman hold anything over you.

My hands slid up her sides and I pinned her wrist above her head.

At least I have some control in here.

"Again?" she asked in sheer disbelief, the corner of her mouth curling into a smirk.

"Again," I growled and buried myself in my happy place.

***

"But I asked you if you needed any help," Mr. Paul said in our morning meeting, his face growing red. "I thought this contract was simple? A done deal?"

"I still believe it is, sir. Bottom line, Clint just needs some extra finessing. But trust me, he is well aware of the incentives and benefits to working with us."

He played with the ballpoint pen on his desk, flustering under the stress. "What if other firms are courting him?"

I shrugged. "They'd be stupid not to. Clint is one of the hottest players in the MLB, probably a major target for most firms. But it's more than courting to him. He needs to feel comfortable. I'm giving him the space but remaining ever-present."

The truth: Clint was a hard man to catch up with. After having to cancel our dinner plans, I had a hard time reaching him, which I assumed his cock-blocking idiot manager had something to do with it.

Mr. Paul shook his head. "I'm not sure about this, Braxton. This isn't how we usually handle business."

"As I'm sure you're well aware, special circumstances require some unconventional methods."

He rubbed his chin, thinking it over.

"Perhaps I should send Miller to maybe just talk with Clint. Like a second wave of defense."

I remained poised as to not give away how much I wanted to flip the fucking desk over at the insult. I could run laps around Miller and not even break a sweat. He had zero swag to interface with clients like Clint.

Who does this old man think he's talking to?

"I have everything under control," I seethed, promising myself that it wasn't a lie, hating having to answer his meaningless questions. I've brought in, and kept, loads of business for Mr. Paul. I took a few months off for my kids and this is the type of disrespect I come back to? He was lucky to still have me!

"I'm serious Braxton. Have this deal done soon or I'll have to transfer it over to someone who doesn't have so much on his plate."

***

Five a.m. Gym.

I needed something to hit so I borrowed some gloves from the front desk. Boxing was the perfect way to relieve stress. Between home life and work life, a few jabs and hooks at a bag was just what I needed. After a quick warm up and a three-mile run, I focused on the heavy bag, then switched to the speed bag until my head started to clear. I had no doubts about my ability to lock Clint as a client, but Mr. Paul sweating me over it, raised some questions within myself about my worth.

Why am I working so hard, taking time away from my children, to make this guy rich and he doesn't even appreciate it?

Then I thought of Brian being home with Ma and his words started coming back to me until the muscles around my neck tightened, almost strangling me.

What does he know about my life with Alexandria? And he better not come fucking near her!

The bag became his head and my jabs intensified until it felt as if my knuckles were bleeding.

"You ok?"

It was the first time I'd heard her voice. Silky, smooth, carefree, the words rolled off her tongue like melted butter. I was so fixed on Brian, I hadn't even notice her move closer, standing behind me in a pink sports bra and matching shorts, skin moist with sweat.

"Yeah," I gasped, wiping the sweat off my forehead.

She eyed me up and down, stopping to stare at my dick like she had x-ray vision then raised an eyebrow.

"You sure?" she purred, hands gripping her thick thighs, head cocked to the side. With her airbrush tan and bright pink lipstick, she reminded me of a porn star, the ones with the bald pussy and vacuum mouths who swallow. I started imagining all the ways I could fuck her in this gym, all the camera angles and the perfect lighting.

She twirled a piece of her long black hair around her finger, waiting. I nodded and smiled, but remained silent. Didn't trust myself. One word and I would've had her ass bent over the ab press machine. She smirked and sashayed back to the free weight area.

I washed up, trying to scrub all the awesomely nasty thoughts out of my brain, and headed out to the car. There was a note on my windshield:

Call me if you ever need a spotter. Natasha.

Damn, even her name was sexy.

***

"Alexandria, we talked about this and you promised to behave yourself."

"I didn't promise that," she snapped. "I said I would be reasonable."

"Is that what you think you're doing right now? Holding our kids hostage in the car is being reasonable?"

Parked outside the children's pediatrician, Dr. Robert Keminski, I made the crucial mistake of jumping out the car before Alexandria. It took a quick twitch of her wrist to lock the doors behind me.

"Alexandria, open the door. I'm not in the mood for this today."

"Neither am I."

"Do you want them to get sick? They need their vaccinations."

Her face crumbled. "Of course I don't want them to get sick! But… can't we wait a little longer? They're just babies!"

Needles had always been an issue for Alexandria. But needles coming towards her children were damn near apocalyptic. Before most checkups, to control her hysteria, I used to feed her valium, hoping it would at least calm her down to a manageable point. But every time, whether it was hysterical crying or near fist fights with the nurses, Alexandria remained impenetrable. In fact, Dr. Keminski was our third pediatrician after some convincing (read: bribing). He had heard about Alexandria. Every doctor in the state of Georgia had heard of her.

"Listen, we've pushed this off long enough. Any longer, they'll call social services."

She peered over her shoulder at the building, hands trembling, tears in her eyes. "Please, Braxton! Don't make me do this. I can't!"

Oh God, not the tears.

I placed a hand on the window because for some strange reason I wanted to hold her.

"Alexandria, would you calm down," I said, in a gentle voice. "They'll be ok. Do you think I would ever put them in harm's way? You know you can trust me."

Alexandria stared at my hand, hesitating.

"Plus," I added. "We'll be there together. We work better as a team. Right?"

She gave me a weak smile with a sniff. Just as she opened her mouth, my Blackberry buzzed. It was Ma.

"Ma," I answered quick, walking away from the car. "You ok? Is something wrong?"

"Braxton," she snapped. "What did you say to Brian?"

Uh-oh.

"What do you mean? I have no idea what you're talking about."

"Did you really tell him that your father didn't want him? That you threatened him to keep away from us, and that's why he doesn't come around anymore?"

Fuck!

"That's not exactly what I said."

"You had no right to do that," she said, her voice trembling. "And you know Brian is having a hard time adjusting. He is trying to change and you're not helping by making it harder on him—ruining his self-confidence. Not everyone can be as blessed as you."

I rubbed my temple and looked back at the car. Alexandria watched, worried.

"Ma, can you please calm down," I said, hitting her with practicality. "This isn't good for your heart."

"Boy, don't treat me like a child!"

"I'm not, MA! I'm just saying, you shouldn't be worried about Brian. He's a grown man, he should be taking care of himself."

"As long as there is breath in my body, I'm always gonna worry and take care of my children. You included! Don't you remember last year, when you asked me to help you with Alex, before she had the babies? Everyone could use a little help sometime."

She just had to bring that up. Throw it in my face, the one time I needed her help. Alexandria had run away and wasn't taking care of herself. So I turned to the one person I could trust. And she was trying to compare that to Brian's inconsequential bullshit?

"Ma," I said, trying not to raise my voice. "Pops was robbing you blind! Someone had to put a stop to him. I thought you would at least appreciate that!"

"You know you're acting just like your father with all this controlling nonsense. I didn't raise you to be cruel!"

Now she's gone too far.

"Fine, Ma! Would you rather Brian took care of you now, since he's so much better than me?"

"Humph, I'll call you back when you calm down." She hung up without saying goodbye. Nothing fries my blood more than being hung up on.

Alexandria, eyes wide and nervous, rolled down the window as I approached.

"Is everything alright?"

"It's fine," I snapped. "Now get the kids out of the car so we can get this over with."

Alexandria pouted, glancing at the sleeping kids in the back seat of the van.

"They're sleeping. Let's just let them sleep. We can do this another day."

"Of course they're fucking sleeping! They're just like their mother and fall asleep whenever they're in the car for more than ten minutes." Her face paled and dropped but I didn't give a shit. I was no longer in the mood for her childish antics.

"Why can't we just do this next week," she pleaded. "I'm not ready!"

I took a breath, preparing for the worst. *Might as well get this over with.*

"Because I won't be here next week. I'm leaving for D.C. tomorrow."

Alexandria froze, and then her eyebrows pinched together before she snorted. She grabbed the keys and stepped out the car, softly closing the door behind her.

"Un-fucking believable," she screamed. "You're going away? Again?"

I rubbed my eyes, willing myself not to snap.

"Alexandria, I need to wrap up this contract with Clint. Plus, be there for the closing on the house."

"This is ridiculous! How could you make these types of plans without discussing it with me first? When exactly were you going to tell me you were heading to D.C.? Were you going to call me from the plane?"

"Listen, I'm not in the mood for this. You think I want to be away from you and the kids?"

"Yes. Yes, actually I do."

The words were like two right hooks to the chin. Enough for me to take a step back to recover. How could she have thought I was TRYING to be away from her and the kids? If she'd only known how much I wanted to go back to the days when it was just us and how I'd give anything to have that time back. She could be so fucking blind sometimes.

"Well, as usual, you don't know anything! You're just as fucking clueless as the day I met you! All I fucking do it take care of your ass and you don't even realize how good you have it!"

She flinched as if a gun shot off, her mouth dropping. I shouldn't have said that. I knew that the moment her head lowered.

Damn it!

Her mouth set into a firm line as I struggled to find the right words to say.

"Listen, I didn't–"

"Don't," she snapped, raising a finger. "Don't say shit to me! It's fine. I'm glad to know you feel as unappreciated as I do. Glad to know we have something in common, for a change."

She crossed her arms, seething in rage.

"Well, let's get this over with," she barked. "The sooner we torture your children, the sooner you can get home and leave us. Just the way you like it!"

She stormed back to the car and that guilty feeling was back, pinching at my chest, making it hard to breathe.

CHAPTER 8

"Thanks for picking me up."

"Thanks for actually telling me you were coming this time," Tiffany said, behind the wheel of her black Acura, driving away from Reagan International Airport towards the twinkling lights of downtown D.C.

I smirked. "I've learned that you don't like surprises."

"I love surprises, especially the good ones," she said with that grin that could make me give her whatever she wanted. I relished the calm drive on the empty highways—chauffeured by a beautiful woman. After a night of arguing with Alexandria, I was ready to be with just about any woman except her.

Tiffany took me straight to her studio apartment in the Adams Morgan section of the city, down the block from the row of restaurants and bars.

"Here we are! Make yourself comfortable," she said, as we entered the cramped space.

There was a futon in the living room that reminded me of my apartment in college, with a decent size TV, a few random pieces of art, and a huge bookshelf, with tan carpeting throughout. A dining room table for two sat outside a narrow opened kitchen with standard white appliances, yellowed from age.

"Nice place you got here," I lied, leaving my bag at the door.

"Thanks," she said, turning on the lights in the kitchen. "But it's not as nice as my new home is going to be."

"Straight to business," I laughed, sitting at the table.

"Only way to handle you tricky salesmen," she said with a wink, pulling some bowls out the fridge. "By the way, did you hear from my attorney yet?"

"Yup, Kevin said he'll drop the sales contract off tomorrow to my hotel. Then, we can both sign it."

"Cool! I'm so excited! Ok, dinner will be ready in a bit."

Tiffany said she was making shrimp Alfredo with a mixed green salad and fresh garlic bread. It sounded fancy, but as I observed her preparing it, it was everything but. She thawed out a tray of pre-cooked shrimp, sprinkled them with salt and pepper, popped open a jar of thick Alfredo sauce, dumped out a bag of pre-washed salad, and broiled some frozen slices of garlic Texas toast.

Alexandria would have at least attempted to make the sauce herself.

I checked my phone. No missed calls from her. I stood, idly rubbing my hands.

"Got any music?"

She nodded. "You can find a music channel on the TV."

I turned on the TV and flipped through, stopping on Sports Center. A repeat, counting down the best baseball plays of last season—Clint being number two. Damn, dude was ferocious on the diamond. He had the potential to be one of the biggest stars of the MLB. Marketed and managed properly, his star power could rocket him to fame.

Just need to convince him of that.

"Okay! Dinner's ready!"

After changing the channel to some classic R&B and lighting a few candles, we sat for our late night meal and I, once again, relished the soothing, relaxing environment. I couldn't remember the last time I had such a peaceful dinner. But then I looked down, expecting a walker to bump into my chair at any moment, feeling the sting of disappointment when it didn't.

"What are you looking at?" Tiffany asked.

I cleared my throat and shook my head. "Nothing."

"You seem distracted," she said, twirling her pasta.

"As they say, lots on my plate."

"Oh yeah, tell me about it?"

She sucks a shrimp off her fork, making it look tastier than it actually was. I shifted in my seat to calm my dick down.

"How about you tell me a little more about you," I said and opened the bottle of wine on the table, my classic deflection move.

"Me? Well, you already know most of it. My life is pretty boring. School, TV production, and writing."

"Come on, you're more exciting than that."

She chuckled. "Wish my ex thought of me as highly as you do. Maybe he wouldn't have cheated."

The word "cheating" shot a quick jab at my stomach. I cleared my throat and poured myself more wine.

"Why don't you tell me about this asshole?"

Another serving of weak pasta and three bottles of red wine later, we were on the floor of her living room: drunk, laughing, joking, listening to late-90's R&B. Simple. That's how it felt hanging with Tiffany. No drama, no nagging or insanity; the definition of a breath of fresh air with her provocative laugh and carefree vibe. Yeah, I felt relaxed, but not totally at ease. I checked my phone again, still no call from Alexandria.

Damn, isn't she worried about me at all?

"You know my home girl told me about you," Tiffany said, lips curling around her empty glass. "You guys went to school together."

"Really," I said, and poured her more wine. "Do tell. What does this friend allegedly know about me?"

"She said you seemed so much older than everyone else. That you were very... intense and focused. Would look straight through people but could still be very charming."

Not surprising her friend would make that observation. The kids I went school with had their parents paying for their education, walking around campus in high price clothing. Focused on parties, clubs, basketball games, Spring Break trips to Miami, and fraternities. I didn't have that luxury. I worked two jobs all throughout my four years, always sending money home for Ma, keeping my background a secret, not out of shame or remorse, but out of pity for those who couldn't possibly understand what my world was like. They lived a sheltered existence; I was a man wise beyond my years and had no time for the chicks throwing themselves at me. When I met Rachel, I was in awe of her brilliance, maturity and innocence. Who could've guessed what she'd turn into?

"Different strokes for different folks, as they say."

"She also said you were a very smooth talker when you wanted something."

I chuckled. "This 'friend' of yours sounds like someone with some leftover bitterness."

"So, is she lying?" Tiffany challenged.

I sighed. "I'll admit... I may have come across as cold sometimes. And I'll take charming as a compliment. But isn't everyone a bit charming when they want something?" My voice lowered and I stared into her big eyes.

"Come to think of it, you're rather charismatic yourself. So what do you want?"

Moving my hand an inch, I touched the tips of her fingers and a static shock electrified us against the carpet. She gasped, our eyes locking, drinking each other in.

"Ummmm… whew! It's hot in here," Tiffany said and stripped out of her sweatshirt. She had on a long white tank top and black leggings, casual yet sexy, right down to her red toes. I sipped more wine hoping that whatever happened, I could just blame on the alcohol.

"Anyway, where were we?" she asked, scooting a little closer on the floor, shaking her hair free of its ponytail.

"I was saying I'm not as cold-blooded as people think. Just focused."

"Hmmm… I think you have time for what you want to have time for."

Fair point.

"And back then, I didn't have time for every woman who wanted my time. Can't be penalized for that," I said, finishing my glass.

"True," she said, her eyes hooded. "Maybe you were just waiting for the right woman."

"Maybe I still am," I said.

Her lips looked delicious, irresistible, probably tasted like the savory wine that was making my head so cloudy.

One kiss couldn't hurt.

Without thinking, I hooked my hand around her neck, bringing her closer, tracing her jaw with my lips. She gasped and let out a little pant, tilting her head down, lips almost meeting mine. And just as I was about to go in for the kill, there was a buzzing. I thought it was just in my head but it was coming from my pocket.

Oh shit, my phone!

I pulled back, scrambling to grab my phone. Tiffany, leaning so far forward, almost fell on her face.

"Whoa. Sorry! I… have to get this. It may be important."

Pissed, she scooted away from me as I jumped up, crossing the room at an attempt at a little privacy.

"Hello! Hello," I answered without even looking at the caller ID.

"Hey, man! What's up, it's Clint." A huge knot of disappointment lumped in my throat, leaving me confused and baffled by Alexandria's audacity.

Is she really not going to return my fucking calls?

"Hello? B? You there?"

I cleared my throat. "Hey, man, good to hear from you."

"I heard you were in town. I'm heading to a party at LIV. You wanna meet up there?"

Another party? Damn.

I glanced over at Tiffany, studying me from her spot on the floor. As much as I wanted to smash her, I needed to lock the deal with Clint. Couldn't get my ass chewed out by Mr. Paul again.

"Uh, yeah. Meet you there," I said and hung up.

Tiffany frowned. "Going somewhere?"

"Yeah. That was my client," I said, looking up the number to a cab. "I've got to go. It's business but I shouldn't be long."

"Oh," she said, her voice flat, trying to check her emotions. "Well, are you coming back?"

"Yeah," I lied.

She shrugged, trying to look unbothered.

"Well, I guess I'll wait up for you."

***

"Aye! What up, man, you're just in time," Clint said, opening up the door to his hotel suite. "I got a serious decision I need your help with."

"Sure," I said, wincing as I entered the sun drenched room while nursing a bottle of Gatorade. Another night with Clint left me hurting, ready to unscrew my head and put it in a freezer. No idea how his liver was still functional with the amount of alcohol he consumed.

Right after my meeting with Mr. Paul, I had called Clint's girlfriend and told her the situation with his bogus manager. She scheduled for us to have a meeting, promising at least an hour for me to make my pitch. I had Sharlene book us both suites at the W Hotel near the White House. It was the best way to get him alone.

"Yo, you were a wild boy last night, B! Didn't know you had it in you!"

"Well I had to come out of retirement and show you young boys how it's done," I said, laughing but longing for my bed, needing at least another ten hours of sleep. I never made it back to Tiffany's—I wasn't even sure how I made it to my hotel alive. But, after I had gotten out of the shower the next morning, I saw her three missed calls and I texted her back:

Got caught up last night. I have the final contract for the house. Meet at my hotel to celebrate?

She texted back, her attitude evident:

Sure.

One word answers from women were never a good sign.

I followed Clint into the living room where an old salt and pepper haired Italian mafia-looking dude was sitting on the sofa. Spread out on the coffee table were two large display briefcases of diamond rings.

"Braxton, this is Turks. Turks, this is my homeboy."

Turks and I shook hands and sat around the boxes. There was at least $500K sitting on the table.

"Aight, Cuz', which one do you like best," Clint said, pointing to two rings sitting on a black velvet cloth. "This one or this one?"

Both were massive diamonds, one oval in shape, the other square, both in diamond-encrusted bands. I didn't know much about rings, but I knew expensive when I saw it.

"Hmmm… this is a tough one," I said. "Which one do you think she'll like?"

He shrugged. "I don't know. She's not very picky."

"Does she like flowers, hearts, candy, and all that Valentine's Day stuff?"

Clint laughed. "Yeah, she's big into that."

I pointed to the oval ring. "Then get her that one. Very soft and romantic."

He grinned and picked up the oval one, examining it, then nodded at the jeweler.

"The man knows the ladies! I'll take this one, Cuz'."

"Excellent choice," Turks said. "Let me package that right up for you." He turned to me. "Care to take a look at one?"

I shook my head. "No thanks, not really my speed."

Clint laughed, while pouring himself a glass of champagne.

"Man, just take a look! Turks is the best in the business. What, you ain't planning on getting married ever?"

I decided to leave Alexandria and the kids out of the conversation for the time being.

"It's a serious commitment," I said, leaning back in my chair. "And an expensive one! You can't be flippant with these types of decisions. You have to be practical."

"Damn, Cuz'. You act like it's a business transaction."

#4 Treat everything like a business. Even love.

"When it boils down to it, everything is business."

"Ha, not everything! Ain't nothing 'practical' about love."

"Love… has its various forms," I chuckled, glancing at the box of rings. "But this is a serious decision. How do you know you're ready? Career wise, you're about to blow up! And more money means more women coming in your direction. Why would you lock yourself down before experiencing some of the finer things in life?"

Clint laughed. "Man, I've seen enough! And ain't nothing out there worth losing Jade over. Plus, she's pregnant. Might as well lock her down, since I'll already be on lock down. Babies got a way of changing the game."

Absolutely.

I thought of Alexandria and groaned. She hadn't answered her phone in two days, so even if I wanted to apologize she had made it impossible. She was being unreasonable, but I still kind of missed her voice.

"You got a lady?" Clint asked, noticing my pensiveness.

"When she feels like being a lady, yeah I got one," I said. "Fucking drives me crazy."

"That's what they're supposed to do! If they didn't drive you crazy, you'd know you didn't give a shit about them."

That made so much fucking sense at that moment that I was shocked no one had ever mentioned it before. I glanced over at the rings again, one catching my eye, sparkling and winking at me in the mid-day sun.

"But… how do you know if you truly found the one?"

Clint poured himself another glass while Turks finished boxing up the ring and writing the receipt.

"I met Jade when I had *nothing*. Didn't even have a car to get to practice. Was still living at my Mom's crib. Jade didn't know nothing about baseball. You show her batting averages and she think she's looking at stock market numbers. But through all my shit, Jade has been there for me. Always looking out for me, always having my best interests at heart. She takes care of me, makes me laugh, and doesn't ask for a thing. All she wants is me. Not saying shit's been easy. She can definitely get on my fucking nerves sometimes. But my Daddy once said, 'When you find a woman like that, someone you can't stand, but can't stand to be without, that's the one for you.' And I can't live without Jade. She's my family now, nothing else matters."

Family?

I had never considered Alexandria family. Sure, she was the mother to my children, but family? It would be putting her in the same category as my Ma, my sisters… that was an exceptional title to bestow on someone, especially someone that liked to give me ulcers for fun.

"And she's smart too," Clint said. "She was the one that found you, remember?"

"Oh yeah. Remind me to buy Jade a nice wedding gift as a thank you. Speaking of which, have you made any decisions yet?"

Clint laughed. "Man, you really are all business. Surprised you don't have your own company or something. I'd love to have you as my manager."

"Not going to lie and say I haven't thought of it," I chuckled.

"So, what's stopping you?" Clint asked. I shrugged, because I really didn't know. "Well, if Jade trusts you, than I trust you."

We laughed and shook hands. I texted Sharlene to email the contract to Jade, bypassing Clint's manager. Turks wrapped up the ring while Clint signed insurance papers. That damn ring was winking at me, again. Turks, never missing a beat of our conversation, eyeballed my every move.

"Do you know your lady's ring size?" he asked, eager to make another sale.

That was an easy question. I knew every square inch of Alexandria's body, from her hair follicles down to her pinky toe. I knew Alexandria better than I knew myself.

"Matter of fact, I do."

***

"Chocolate martini. Your favorite, right?" I had Tiffany's drink ready at the hotel bar when she approached, dressed in a tight red skirt and a white off the shoulder top, with pretty gold heels.

"Is this your way of apologizing?" she said, pretending to be annoyed but failing.

"Sort of. Actually, I'm hoping this will make up for the… misunderstanding," I said, pulling the sales contract out of my gray blazer.

Her eyes lit up and she clapped with a shriek.

"Yay! Oh thank you, thank you, thank you," she said, jumping out of her seat to hug me.

"Don't mention it," I said, laying the contract out on the counter and placing my ballpoint pen on top.

She gushed over the paperwork. "Wow, I'm going to be a home owner. I can't believe it."

"Yup. All you have to do is sign."

She nodded and folded up the contract, slipping it in her bag with my pen.

What the hell is she doing?

"I'll sign it later. AFTER we celebrate!"

"I thought we were celebrating now?"

She shook her head. "Nope. I want the type of celebration that involves champagne, shots, and lots of dancing!"

"Umm, actually, I'm pretty tired and I…"

"Don't be such an old man," she said, waving me off. "Plus, you owe me from last night."

My body couldn't take another night out partying. Plus, I still hadn't heard from Alexandria. Couldn't believe she was being this fucking bull-headed. Even for her, this was excessive. Ignoring me, as if she didn't miss me at all!

"So," Tiffany said, sipping her drink. "What'll it be?"

I checked my phone again. No missed calls. I sighed, turned it off, and smiled at her.

"Ladies choice!"

We ended up at a lounge close to the hotel. We didn't even have our coats off before walking straight to the bar.

"Shots, please," she said to the bartender.

"Shots? Don't you want to start off slow?"

"We're celebrating! Whoo-hoo!"

Exhaustion kicked in and I fought back a yawn. "Don't you get tired of partying?"

"Braxton, we're young! Leave that talk to the old married-with-kids folk."

I faked a laugh, as the bartender brought us two lemon drop shots.

Six shots later, the place was packed, and we were so far gone—dancing hard, popping bottles, jumping on couches. Every song was her song. And every song made me want to dance with her. I loved the way her ass backed into my dick, the way she danced with her eyes closed, head leaning back against my chest. I loved how loose she was, like she didn't have a care in the world. And for the first time in a long time, I felt... free. Nothing tying me down. No nagging bitching girlfriends, no stress of trying to take care of Ma, no exams to study for, no bosses to answer to, no responsibilities. I was weightless and limitless.

I didn't know if it was just the moment, or if it was Tiffany making me feel this way. I didn't know if it was just the change of scenery, or the alcohol that made me start questioning myself. Like, what if I had met this girl sooner? Would my life have been different? She was so vibrant, full of joy, and magic.

The way Alexandria used to be.

My stomach heaved into my chest and my lungs squeezed shut. I pretended it was just alcohol making me want to puke and not the thought of my wife. I refused to believe she had that type of effect on me. No woman had that type of effect on me.

I'm Braxton Fucking Earwood!

But the lights and music were making my head spin. I needed some air or I was going to pass out.

"Let's get out of here," I said in Tiffany's ear.

She gave me an eager nod with a drunken grin and I led her to coat check. Outside, waiting for our taxi, air returned to my lungs and I laughed off my mini panic attack. Tiffany was staring at me with these wanton eyes, licking her red lips, hungry. I couldn't remember the last time a woman made me feel so desired in all the right ways. My head was foggy but one thing was clear: Life would have been so different if I had met Tiffany first.

Still can be different.

"Sooo… I don't know about you," Tiffany said, as the cab pulled up. "But I plan on having sex tonight."

Whoa.

"Uh, ok," I said feigning innocence.

A smile crept up on her face. "And I plan on having it with you."

And just like that, my dick and the alcohol took over the conversation.

"Well, since you put it that way…"

***

For a split second, I was confused about where I was. Yes, I was in my hotel room, in my bed. But there was a woman draped around me. And she wasn't Alexandria. I didn't know what made the scene more nauseating: the empty champagne bottles on the desk, the clothes scattered on the floor, or the condom wrappers on the nightstand.

Tiffany stirred in my arms and looked up at me, smiling.

"Good morning," she yawned, with a small stretch. "Sleep okay?"

I shrugged. "Yeah."

Her head popped up, measuring the tone in my voice. "What's wrong?"

Suddenly, it didn't feel right having her in my arms. It felt fucking weird.

"Nothing… just got a busy day ahead of me," I said, trying not to stutter. "Meetings and stuff. Actually, I should probably get started."

I slipped from under her and grabbed my clothes out the closet. Tiffany sat up and brought the covers up to her chin.

"Are you sure you're okay?" she asked, sounding hurt.

Damn, B, don't be a complete asshole about this.

"Yeah," I said with a smile. "I'm just gonna jump in the shower real quick. Be right back."

Tiffany nodded as I rushed into the bathroom, desperate to be alone.

Shit. What have I done?

Usually after sex, I felt refreshed, rejuvenated with a lighter load for my dick to carry. Standing in the shower, I waited, but felt none of those things. Guilt was sucking me lifeless and numb. Although I had flirted heavily in the past and came damn close to it, I had never actually cheated on Alexandria before. Never really stepped out on her.

I thought fucking Tiffany would have brought back some of the old me. That maybe I could fight the power Alexandria had over me. But I hated the club scene, the non-stop partying, and the hangovers. I was over this stage in my life, and Tiffany was still stuck in it. There wasn't even anything memorable about sex with Tiffany, nothing worth this contrition. That raging fire I had with Alexandria, it was missing. It was like being on heroin, forced to slum back down to weed. And the withdrawal left me feigning for my wife.

Shit. What have I done?

Showered and dressed, I came out the bathroom and Tiffany was in a hotel robe, watching cartoons.

"Great! My turn," she said, grabbing her clothes off the floor. "Hey, do you want to grab breakfast downstairs real quick, before you start your day?"

I smiled. "Yeah, sure. Sounds like a great idea."

"Cool," she said and skipped into the bathroom.

How am I going to break it off with this chick? She's too damn sweet.

I turned on my phone while considering my options. I couldn't just fade to black on her, and I doubted that she'd accept this as a one night stand. I had to give some type of explanation. *But maybe I could hold on to her, just for a little while longer.* Who knew if this thing with Alexandria would be there forever! I could fly back to D.C. a couple of times a year, no one would be the wiser.

Shit, I'm an asshole for even considering this. No! I have to break it off.

The phone wasn't even on a second before it rang. It was Alexandria.

Oh shit... does she know?

For a split second I panicked then reassessed. No possible way, I was careful about all the places we went to and covered up my tracks. Shit, even acknowledging that made me fucking scum.

Tiffany hummed in the shower, and against my better judgment, I answered the call.

"Where have you been? I've been calling you since yesterday!"

Shit.

"Good morning to you, too," I said, never missing an opportunity to be a smart ass. "My phone died and I lost my charger."

"For fuck's sake, Braxton! Just… when are you coming home?"

"Tomorrow night," I said, keeping my voice low. "Why, what's up?"

"Mia's sick, and of course got the kids sick in the process. You need to come home. Now!"

The water turned off in the bathroom. I moved to the other side of the room.

"I can't right now," I whispered. "I haven't–"

"I don't give a fuck!"

The kids fussed and cried on the other end of the line. Alexandria tried to comfort them but they sounded miserable. With a groan, I grabbed my bag out of the closet and threw it on the bed.

"What's wrong with them?" I mumbled, low enough so Tiffany couldn't hear.

"Everything! They all have fevers AND diarrhea. I'm covered in shit. Literally."

"Did you take them to the doctor?"

"I only have two hands here, Braxton. And in case you've been under a rock, doctors don't make house calls. I can't do this by myself."

I breathed in deep to keep myself from snapping at her. Tiffany emerged from the bathroom, wrapped in a towel. Her skin still slightly moist and her hair wrapped in a bun. She smiled as she walked over to the bed.

She's the worst type of distraction.

I rushed into the bathroom to keep the conversation private, packing up my toiletries. There was a loud splatter and Alexandria moaned.

"Shit, Alex threw up. Awww, baby, it's ok! Mommy's got you. Braxton, I've gotta go! Come home now! I mean it!"

Who the fuck does she think she is, ordering me around?

"What do you want me to do? Just lose this client all together?"

"Fuck your client! Is he more important than your kids? Look, I've been pretty goddamned understanding but now you're being an ass. Your kids need you! So you better be on the next fucking plane!"

I wanted to correct her for using such language around the children but the line went dead.

Fucking hate it when she hangs up on me!

Knowing Alexandria's wild imagination, I suspected the kids probably weren't as bad as they seemed. But the four of them sick together was surely overwhelming. She was right though. I'm fucking around with some chick while my kids needed me.

Damn, I really am turning into my Pops.

That tingling guilt feeling returned, pinching my stomach worse than before. I walked out the bathroom and stopped short. Tiffany laid across the bed, dressed, playing with the zippers on my duffle bag.

"Going somewhere?" she asked with a grin.

Trying not to panic, I relaxed my tense stance and sauntered to the desk, avoiding eye contact.

"I got an emergency. I have to go back to Atlanta." I grabbed my tie off the chair and raised the collar of my shirt in the mirror.

"Oh, damn," she said, sitting up. "Everything okay?"

"Yeah, I'm sure everything is fine," I said, trying not to stare at her playing with my bag, praying she would stop.

"Well, here, let me help you pack so we can get out of here before checkout."

She grabbed the duffle bag and it toppled over on the floor. The black velvet ring box rolled out the side pocket, landing in the middle of the room.

Shit.

Tiffany froze, staring like it was an unknown predator about to attack her.

"What... what's that?"

I tried to cross the room swiftly and scoop the box up before she could react any further, but she bent forward and picked it up with ease. She examined the box, rotating it like a Rubric's Cube before opening it. Her eyes bulged as she gasped. The ring was meant to take Alexandria's breath away, not hers.

"It's an engagement ring," she said flatly.

With a sigh, I turned back to the mirror and continued to straighten my tie. The key was not to react like something was unusual.

"Yes, it is."

She sat silent for another thirty seconds.

"Why... why do you have one?"

Digging through my toiletry bag, I grabbed my brush, letting my silence do the talking. "Why the hell do you have a ring, Braxton?" she repeated, her squeaky voice raising another octave.

I don't remember asking her to pick up my bag. And who the hell does she think she's talking to like that?

I did what I to do best and flipped the script. "For the record, I don't appreciate you going through my personal belongings as if they were your own. It's not a good look."

Stunned by my words, she blinked a couple of times to gain her composure.

"Why do you have a ring?" she asked again, shaking the box at me.

"That's none of your concern."

"Ummm... we just made love. I think I have a right to know."

Love? Is that what she thinks we just did? No wonder she was being so nonsensical. She was delusional.

Just like Alexandria was.

This only confirmed my resolve to ignore her tirade further. I learned a long time ago, you can never win an argument with an insane woman. Tiffany stood flabbergasted by my unresponsiveness.

"Sooo... let me get this straight," she started, staring at me through the mirror. "You have a girlfriend?"

"Something like that."

That wasn't a lie. She just wasn't asking the right questions.

"Something like what? You either do or you don't," she snapped.

"Then no, I don't have a girlfriend," I said plainly.

I might as well get this over with.

"I have a wife. A wife and four children."

It took her a moment to catch her breath, and what little color she had drained from her face, Her eyes blinked once before stretching wide. She shook her head, falling back on to the bed, her knees giving out on her.

"I'm... I'm sorry I must have misheard you. Did you say FOUR children?"

"Yes," I said while moving about the room, repacking the duffle that had fallen on the floor. "Four. Quadruplets to be exact."

"Quad... I... I don't... understand," she muttered in disbelief.

Sure, I could've lied. I could've told her I was holding the ring for one of my boys who was preparing to propose to his girlfriend. I could've created a litany of explanations. But there was no use in delaying the inevitable. I had no plans nor desire to carry out some type of long distance, extramarital affair. Tiffany would have found out eventually. Better the story comes direct from the horse's mouth.

"You never told me," she said, sounding wounded.

"You never asked."

She gagged, revolted by me, and dropped the box on the floor. I scooped it up, making sure the ring was still in place.

"I didn't think I would have to ASK," she screamed, storming across the room. I stuffed the ring in my briefcase as she gathered her purse and jacket, heading towards the door. She stopped short, turning back with the contract in her hand and ripped it to pieces, throwing it at my chest.

I sighed. "I take it the deal is off?"

With an icy stare, she stomped out the room, slamming the door behind her.

***

"You know you did it to yourself. You let that shit go too far," Kevin said, driving towards the airport.

"Thanks for pointing out the obvious."

"Anytime, dickhead. So you think the deal is done?"

"Pretty much," I sighed. He kept quiet and I was grateful. I didn't need the 'I told you so speech.' I already felt pretty shitty. Neither one of us wanted to shell out another mortgage payment on a dead property. I let him down. Fuck, I let myself down too.

Kevin pulled up to the departure gate with a sigh.

"I'll take care of it," he said. "Just don't fuck the next one. Ok?"

I rolled my eyes and headed for check in. It cost five hundred dollars to reschedule my flight and almost an hour to get through security. With the lack of sleep, the pounding headache, and an angry email from Mr. Paul, the day just kept getting better and better.

Walking towards my gate, I stopped at the newsstand to grab some aspirin and a men's health magazine for my flight. At the checkout counter, a little Indian woman was staring at my every movement. Used to being profiled, I didn't pay her much attention, until she finally snapped her fingers.

"I know you! Yes, you on cover of magazine!"

"Sorry, I think you're mistaken," I said with a sigh, assuming it was one of those 'all black people lookalike' situations.

"No, no! Look. This way, come."

I followed the little woman to the corner of store where the family magazines were kept. On the middle shelf, was the new issue of *Parents* magazine with the kids, Alexandria and I on the cover.

"This just come yesterday," she said, beaming proud. "Yes, that's you, right?"

"Holy shit," I mumbled, dropping my bag and grabbing a copy. "That IS me!"

It was the perfect family portrait: The kids in their matching outfits, a bunch of smiling, happy babies. And then Alexandria and I, with her head on my shoulder and my arm wrapped around her waist, glowing, natural, and comfortable. I was taken aback by how happy we looked.

The morning of the photo shoot, we had spent an hour playing peek-a-boo at the breakfast table while Alexandria made my favorite pancakes. On the car ride over, the kids danced in their seats to Stevie Wonder. And at bedtime, before we read *Goodnight Moon*, I played the tickle monster, even with Alexandria. I'd give anything to hear their giggles right now.

With so much drama over the last couple of weeks, I almost forgot how simple life could to be with just the six of us, even in the hectic chaos that is our home. I forgot how my kids made me happy. How Alexandria made me happy, even when she drove me crazy. Some days I wanted to strangle her and others I wanted to kiss the hell out of her.

There was no reason to chase my old life, my legacy, when I had a perfect life back home.

With my family.

CHAPTER 9

There was an unfamiliar car in the driveway when I pulled in.

Who the fuck is this?

Between the delayed flights, traffic jams, and lost baggage, I was ready for an uninterrupted climb into bed, maybe some head—not company.

I entered the house and slammed the door behind me. Sasha approached, but sensed my mood and backed away whimpering. A deep bass of an unrecognizable man's voice echoed from the living room. I crept in slow, giving my blood time to simmer down, but it only boiled more at the scene: Alexandria on the couch, dressed in a thin low cut tank top and pink sweat pants; next to her, some dark skin dude with cornrows; in his lap, Aiden.

"Hey! You came home," Alexandria beamed.

My fist balled up. "Is that allowed?"

The dude raised an eyebrow and quickly handed Aiden over to Alexandria. He wasn't oblivious, unlike my fucking wife. He stood, crossing the living room in two quick strides.

"Aye man, what's up, I'm Akir." He extended a hand and I ignored it. His mischievous smile was unsettling, mocking. His hat was cocked to the side, jeans half on, belt loosely buckled.

What the fuck's been going on in here?

Alexandria stood up behind him. She frowned and mouthed a "stop it" over his shoulder. Her hair seemed out of place, disheveled and her face moist, as if she had been sweating.

Sweating doing what?

I stood rigid, breathing out my nose, trying to hold it together but thinking of my gun upstairs. Akir dropped his hand while Alexandria piped in.

"So Akir is in town and stopped by to say hello but got more than he bargained for. I put him to work as soon as he walked in the door. He helped me get the kids to bed and hung on to Aiden while I cleaned up. You should have seen this place, it was a nightmare!"

I said nothing. The story only added fuel to the flame.

"Oooook then," Akir chuckled and turned to Alexandria, staring at me as if I was a complicated calculus equation. "So, Alex, I think I'mma take off."

Alexandria shook herself out of her trance and refocused.

"Uhh, yeah… okay," she said, giving me another curious glance. "I'll walk you to the door."

Akir turned to me again and raised an eyebrow. "Well, later."

He smirked before slipping by me, walking towards the door with a stupid purposeful limp. Alexandria placed Aiden in my arm before rolling her eyes.

"I'll be right back," she mumbled and rushed behind him. Aiden stared up at me, expressionless, as if there was no recognition at all, which only amplified my rage.

"I'm sorry about that," Alexandria said to Akir by the door. "He's been under a lot of stress at work, lately."

Yeah, working to take care of your ass while you're home fucking some other dude.

"Nah, it's all good," he said.

"Thanks again for today. You were a really big help today. I really appreciate it."

"No problem, anytime. Like I said, it was good to see you."

"Same here. Thanks again!"

She closed the door and raced back into the living room. I hadn't moved from my spot. I was too focused on controlling my anger with a baby in my hands. But then it happened: the image of Akir fucking Alexandria on my couch with Aiden watching from his playpen burned in brain.

"Well that was rude. What the hell is your problem?" she snapped.

Holding Aiden tighter, I swallowed hard. He was the only thing keeping me from attempting murder.

"Who the fuck was that?" My voice must have reached a new low because her head snapped back.

"I just *told* you, that was Akir. A friend from college."

A friend? Tiffany was a friend too.

"I've never heard of him."

"I didn't think I had to mention every friend I've ever had."

"Now is not a good time for your smart ass mouth! What the fuck was he doing here?"

Her mouth dropped as she struggled to defend herself.

"He… was in town visiting. He got my number from Kennedy and called me up last minute, wanting to stop by."

Kennedy. Of course.

Aiden fussed in my arms, but I wouldn't let loose of him.

"It's a little late for company, don't you think," I mumbled and stormed towards the kitchen. She trotted behind me.

"What you mean? I was *drowning* in here without you and he offered to help. Jeez, what's wrong? What the hell did I do now? Why are you so goddamned angry? "

I spun around, holding Aiden between us.

"'Cause you had this mutherfucker in MY house when I wasn't here! Holding MY son! Dealing with MY children! You probably don't even know him that well. Not every dude you're friends with has the best intentions. And you sitting here with your breast all out… what was I supposed to think when I walked in here?"

Her mouth dropped, eyes growing wide. Even I was a little shocked by my outburst. I left her frozen and grabbed a bottle out the fridge. The cool air did nothing to extinguish the rage I felt.

After all, he wanted her. What man wouldn't?

Alexandria took a deep breath, and I waited for her storm, ready for the fight.

Another man. In my house. Holding my son. Bitch is fucking crazy.

"You're right," she said.

I stepped out of the fridge, dumbstruck. "Huh?"

She chuckled with a heavy sigh, throwing her hands up in defeat.

"I said, you're right. You're absolutely right. It was wrong of me to have another man in our home without telling you first. I'm sure that's not what you wanted to come home to, especially after I made a fuss about you coming home. I'm sorry."

I tried to hold my stoic glare, but I was shell-shocked.

Is she… apologizing… to me?

She shrugged as her lips curved up into my favorite childlike smile.

"Nothing happened," she said. "If that's what you were thinking. I wouldn't… dare. It's just, I don't have many friends down here, other than you and the kids. So it's nice to have adult company once and a while. I know you've been working hard and under a lot of stress. And it's all to take care of us… you're a good man. Even if you're a jerk sometimes."

Who are you and what have you done with Alexandria?

We stared at each other, eyes fixed, trying to read each other's thoughts. I didn't know how to respond. She seemed different, calm and not her usual frazzled, neurotic self, and not the woman who barked at me on the phone just a few hours ago. We had switched places.

"I… I'm sorry. Did… did I walk into the right house?"

She laughed and scooped Aiden out of my arms.

"Yep. This is the only house on the block with quadruplets in it."

Aiden smiled at me from his mother's arms as she tickled him with her nose.

"You look tired," she said and stroked my face, her hand like silk. "I'm going to take Aiden to bed. Why don't you relax and when I come back down, I'll heat up some dinner."

She gave a rueful smile with a resolving nod, then reached up on her toes and kissed me. Just as she pulled away, I yoked her back, cupping her face, and tonguing her down. I needed her warmth, her familiarity, to feel at home again. She moaned and jerked away, staring at me.

"What?" I asked. "What's wrong?"

She balanced Aiden on her hip, touching her lips. Confused and unsure, she struggled to find her words.

"You… you kissed me… different."

I pressed my lips together, my stomach hitting the floor.

"Weird. I don't know," she continued, as if talking to herself. "It was almost like you've been kissing someone else."

Oh fuck!

She swirled the thought in her head, reasoning with herself. Was it possible, to know someone so intimately that you could tell the slightest change in their behavior? I would have thought she was crazy if she wasn't so dead right. To deny anything would only make me look guilty so I chose to keep silent. Finally, she let out a relieved laughed.

"Ha, I'm sorry. I don't know what's gotten into me. I sound crazy! I've been up all night with these kids. Their fevers broke not too long ago."

I exhaled and laughed with her. A guilty laugh, the kind that felt like jabs to my lungs.

Shit, that was a close one.

"I'll be right back," she said and strolled out the kitchen, murmuring to Aiden, smothering him with kisses. She looked five years older. Hours without sleep and juggling sick children would do that to you, I guess.

I sat at the kitchen nook, holding my head up with my hands. My mind continued to toggle between my paranoid delusions of another man's hands on Alexandria, and the images of Tiffany, her lips on my chest, making their way down my stomach. I could still smell her on me.

Or was that Alexandria?

What burned most was the idea that she had relied on some other man to help take care of MY children; that I wasn't there for her when she needed me. I am an asshole at heart, but I had no right to take my anger out on Alexandria. Not after what I'd done. She could've slept with Akir if she really wanted to, and I would've never known. But she didn't. She had been nothing but loyal, supportive, and catering since I'd known her. I've treated her like shit and then scolded her after coming home from fucking another woman...

I don't deserve her.

I took the stairs three at a time, just as she tiptoed out of the kids' room, softly closing the door behind her.

"What's wrong?" she whispered, smiling at me.

"Come here," I growled.

Her eyes widened before I pounced on her, wrapping her up in my arms with a quick lift, lips crashing into her. She wrapped her legs around my waist.

"Braxton," she moaned.

Her breath quickened as I carried her to our room. We stripped each other, falling on the bed, tangled in heat and need. I flipped her over and rammed into her.

"Ah," she screamed.

"This is mine," I growled, pulling her tighter to me.

"Yes but... ah!"

I pulled her hair and she arched back.

"I don't want anyone touching this but me."

"Braxton, I... ah, ah, ah," she panted.

Grabbing her shoulder, I plunged hard, faster. She screamed into a pillow. Not in pain, but pleasure, as she pulsed and tightened around me.

"Not even a fucking doctor without MY permission," I threatened, knowing how ridiculous it sounded, but the intense desire for possession was fueling every thrust. She glanced over her shoulder, a sexy smile on her lips, sweat glistening on her back, as she pushed against me.

That's my girl.

We were loud: smacking, grabbing, pulling, and scratching; obscene yet delicious. It felt right, felt like home.

***

Five a.m. Gym.

Good sex makes working out a breeze. After a quick warm up, I hit the treadmill for a three-mile run, still grinning. Alexandria always got my heart pumping and ready for more. In fact, I didn't even want to be at the gym, I wanted to be home with her and the kids. So I rushed through three reps of squats, forty-pound free-weights, fifty pull-ups, fifty knuckle push-ups and fifty sit-ups. After a quick stretch, I headed for the showers.

I guess I didn't notice her come in that morning, or maybe I was too focused on the finish line, that I'd forgotten all about Natasha. But she hadn't forgotten about me.

Steam swirled around her as she opened the curtain of my shower stall. I rubbed the shampoo out of my eyes, making sure I wasn't seeing things.

"Natasha?"

She grinned, licking her lips. Frozen stiff, I stared, my mouth hanging open, feeling exposed since…well, I was butt-fucking-naked and she was standing there with her eyes focused on my dick. She smirked, stripping off what little clothes she had on. Her body was as glorious as I pictured it would be: Tight waist, smooth fat ass, flawless skin. The bar of soap fell out of my hand.

Am I fucking dreaming?

She giggled. "You like?"

My heart was racing, my body so in shock I couldn't even speak.

"Ha! I can tell you like," she said and nodded down at my dick, now sprung to action, hard as a rock.

It has a mind of its own, I swear.

Slowly, she dropped to her knees in front of me, her hair soaked and slicked back. I stopped breathing, blinking a few more times to make sure she was real. Her hands, smooth as pearls, began massaging my shaft. My eyes rolled back and I gripped the wall to keep from falling.

Oh fuck!

There she was, her pretty knees on the dark blue tiles, water splashing in her pretty face, as she stared up with those pretty brown eyes, while her pretty lips were opened wide, inching towards me, about to give me what I imagined would be the best fucking head of my life. My fantasy come true.

But in my recent fantasies, it was always Alexandria on her knees, her beautiful eyes staring up at me. And like a bucket of ice water splashed in my face, I woke out of my trance. Natasha was banging, but not everything that sparkles is a diamond. Regal told me that once.

"Stop," I gasped, gripping her shoulder, pulling my dick out of her hands.

She giggled, as if I was playing and reached for me again. I moved, my back against the cold wet wall and her smile dropped.

"I'm… married," I stuttered out, my heart trying to beat out of my chest.

She glanced at my ring finger and snorted. "You sure about that?"

With a deep breath, I nodded. "Very sure."

She stood, shrugged as if to say "your loss" and stepped out the stall, slipping her shirt back on.

HOLY SHIT! That was close.

I exhaled a few deep breaths and turned the water to arctic. On the way out, I stopped at the door, staring at my lone car in the parking lot, thinking of the note Natasha left the last time.

#9 Never catch yourself in a bad situation twice.

I spun back around to the reception desk.

"Hi. I need to cancel my membership."

***

Alexandria, dressed in her robe, her hair in a sloppy bun, was at the stove, stirring a pot of oatmeal with cinnamon and raisins. Not even out of my gym gear, I slipped my arms around her waist, burying myself in her neck, taking a relieving breath.

Who knew being faithful would be so… complicated.

"Morning," she chirped, rubbing my neck. "Say good morning guys!"

The kids slapped on the trays of their high chairs, shrieking happy baby gibberish.

"Morning guys," I said, pulling a chair in front of them. "So, what's for breakfast? You guys like oatmeal?"

Aiden blew raspberries while Brandi cooed.

"Yeah," I laughed. "Me either. My Ma made me eat this stuff too."

Alexandria chuckled behind me and nudged my arm, passing me a bowl and tiny spoon. She knew how I liked to feed the kids before work. It allowed me a few extra moments with them before I disappeared for the day.

"Oh boy, guys, here we go! Breakfast time," I said, stirring their mushy food. "But first, let's try again. Say Da-Da." The kids squealed and grinned, showing their little baby teeth, slapping their hands against their trays. "Aw come on, guys, I know you can do it. Just try. Sayyyyy Da-da."

Brandi reached for the spoon. "Da!"

"Oh, you almost had it! Come on baby girl, one more time! Who am I? I'm Da-Da"

Brandi kicked her foot out, grinning, gnawing on her hand. "Da-da-da-da!"

Oh shit! She did it!

"Ha! Whoo! Did you hear that?!"

But she wasn't paying attention. Alexandria, coffee in one hand, newspaper in the other, was leaning over the kitchen-island, her breasts like two loaves of wheat bread on the counter. The sun peaked through the blinds, landing on her golden skin, highlighting the brown in her hair that fell over her shoulders. She licked her lips, tucked some strands behind her ear and turned the page.

Fuck, she's gorgeous.

It was moments like these that made me remember why I fell for her so hard. Between the insanity, the arguments, and comic relief, whether laughing with her or at her (ok, mostly at her) there was a layer of peace in Alexandria's madness. Peace that I never had with anyone else. Peace was something I spent my entire life searching for. And real talk: finding it, so unexpectedly, scared me… enough to want to push it away sometimes.

Sensing my silence, she glanced up and frowned. "What?"

"What?"

"You're staring at me," she chortled.

Shit.

"No I'm not. Just thinking. Can't I think?"

Wow, she's never caught me staring before.

She shook her head. "You feeling alright? You've been acting so weird lately."

***

"Hey, I'm going to take you out to dinner tonight."

There was a pause on the other end of the phone. "Sorry, I think you dialed the wrong number," Alexandria laughed.

The afternoon sun glimmered off the Atlanta skyline. I'd been staring at it all day, thinking about her. I'd been thinking about her way too much.

"I'm serious. Dinner. Tonight."

"Ok, you're scaring me. You're being way too nice. What have you done? Or wait, are you dying?"

"You would assume that. Can't I just take you out? I've already asked Mia if she could come over to watch the kids. She'll be there around three so you can get ready. She's bringing you a dress I just bought with some of those fancy shoes you like. Wear it. It's a nice place."

"Wow… you put some thought into this," she said over the kids playing and shrieking in the background.

"Don't I always?"

"Not that I'm aware of, actually, no."

Well, she has a point.

"See you at six," I said and hung up, checking my emails one more time.

"Hey, Sharlene?" I called, and she rushed to the door.

"Yes, sir?"

"Have you receive the Clint Davis contract yet?"

"No sir, not yet."

"Hmm… strange. Can you follow up please? I need this wrapped up today."

***

The ring was on fire. It was burning a hole through my slacks, scorching my thigh as I pulled into the driveway. I was tired of carrying it around but excited to see her reaction. I realized that I took great joy and satisfaction in pleasing my woman. *My woman.*

I beeped the horn twice as I waited in the driveway for Alexandria with two-dozen red roses sitting in the passenger seat. Sharlene had reserved a table for two at Bacchanalia, where I had planned to give her the ring, nonchalantly, of course. I didn't want to make a big production out of it.

She'll probably burst into tears. Congratulatory wishes, dinner, followed by the best sex she's ever had or quite possibly the best I've ever had.

But her ring wasn't the one set ablaze. The one giving me third degree burns was my own platinum wedding band. I'd had it customized with four diamonds to represent our four children. With her ring, I was neither nervous nor apprehensive. But a ring for my own hand, yeah, I had much trepidation.

Wearing the ring meant a divorce from my former self, a sacrifice of my anonymity and ambiguous status. I'd played a close hand all my life to keep prying gossipers at bay, and I took much pride in befuddling those around me, which only made them thirstier for more juice on my life. If it weren't for Alexandria having four kids instead of the normal one or maybe two, no one would even have known I had children. But it wasn't Alexandria's fault, and it was time for me to stop punishing her as if it was.

I beeped the horn again, more agitated than before.

What's taking her so long?

The door flung open and Mia ran out, frantically waving her arms. I sprung from the car.

"What's wrong? Are the kids ok?" I shouted, her face pale and nervous, as I flew into the house. The kids were in the living room, sitting on the floor, wearing the same nervous and frightened expression Mia had. They fumbled over each other to reach me and I dove on the floor, inspecting each one for injuries; all were accounted for and fine. Mia stood by, shaking.

"Mia, what's wrong?"

A crash from upstairs made her jump. I stood, inadvertently picking Bethany and Lil' Alex up with me. There were snaps of wood breaking followed by a BOOM! Like someone threw a bowling ball in the air and it landed on the floor above our heads. After another crash, the kids jumped and whimpered.

"What the fuck is going on?" I demanded.

Mia stepped closer to me, as if afraid to be heard.

"I don't know. Some woman called a little while ago asking for Alex," she whispered, eyes glued to the stairs. "She got on the phone and was pretty quiet, then they started arguing. She said your name a couple of times. Then she threw the phone and went upstairs. She's been this way ever since."

I followed her gaze toward a dent in the wall on the other side of the room, the phone shattered into pieces on the floor.

Some woman? Shit.

I kissed Beth and Lil' Alex before placing them back on the floor. They whimpered and Mia rushed over to comfort them.

"Stay with them. Don't come upstairs, no matter what."

Mia nodded and I glanced at the kids. Their tear-soaked faces crumbled into frowns as their lips trembled and they began to cry. They were terrified of their own mother.

Sasha stood outside the closed door of our bedroom, her nose glued to the ground, desperate to sniff inside.

I took a deep breath and flung open the door. If we lived in the Midwest, I would have sworn a tornado had touched down in one particular room of the house. Lamps knocked over, sheets torn, the mattress bare and turned sideways. The closet, almost empty, looked like it had thrown up—clothes were spread around the room. Actually, that's a lie. Only MY clothes were tossed, my button down shirts ripped into shreds. Every drawer opened, papers scattered, books torn. White feathers suspended in the air like snow, the carcass of a pillow by my feet. But nothing compared to the rage in Alexandria's eyes, who was standing in the middle of the room. Sasha blew past me, sniffing her for damages.

A sinister snarl escaped her lips. Whatever she was holding, she dropped with complete disregard.

"Once a cheater, always a cheater. Isn't that what you said?"

Fuck.

I closed the door behind me to keep our conversation isolated, though it wouldn't help much. From the deep tone in her voice, flaring nostrils, and narrowing eyes, it was bound to be a screaming argument. I prayed something, anything, would happen to avoid it: a stroke, a car crash, anything. But nothing did.

"Alexandria, what are you doing? You're scaring the kids," I said, hitting her with practicality, hoping bringing up the children would divert her attention and subdue her anger. She stood glaring. She wasn't falling for it.

"You. Mutherfucking. Bastard. How could you?"

"How could I what?"

"DON'T! Don't you dare try to play STUPID! You KNOW what I'm talking about!"

Pretending to be just as frustrated, I glided my hands down my face with a groan, then stared at her, buying myself time. Her eyes flickered before her lips peeled back into a sarcastic smile.

"Or perhaps there are so many that you don't know which bitch I'm referring to," she chuckled. "Well let me make it easy for you. The writer."

Fuckkkkkkk!

This was bad but I had to be strategic. She had found out, heard directly from the horse's mouth, no denying it. It was time to play the calm, cool, and collected Braxton.

"Alexandria—"

"What? What the fuck kind of bullshit excuse are you gonna give me today? Huh? Did she slip and fall on your dick? Come on, tell me. I'm dying to hear it!"

"Alex–"

"Do you have ANY idea what I have had to deal with? While you're flying around, fucking bitches, I'm here taking care of YOUR children! I've been covered in shit and pissed on. I can barely take a proper shower. I can't do ANYTHING on my own for more than two minutes. Yet you have alllllll the time in the world to fuck other bitches!"

I groaned. "You keep saying bitches like it was more than one. You need to get your facts straight before you accuse me of shit."

Her head snapped back and I immediately knew that I shouldn't have said that.

"See, right there, that's where you're mistaken. I'm not accusing you of anything. Accusing you would mean I was claiming something without proof. I read enough of your law books to know the difference. The evidence just fucking called me and said you and her fucked last weekend. Described your entire dick game, down to the very detail of the face you make when you come."

This was bad—caught couldn't even begin to cover it. Staring at her, I struggled to find the appropriate words to end this tirade.

"Calm down, okay? You're scaring the kids."

"Don't tell me to calm down! And don't pretend to give a damn about them! You stopped caring about them when you decided to fuck that bitch!"

Okay, now she's gone too far.

She was justified in reaming me out for cheating, but questioning my devotion to the kids? That crossed several lines. I stepped towards her, grinding my teeth.

"Alexandria, it is what it is. I can't take it back. It's in the past. You need to get over it."

She raced across the room and laid one earth-shattering slap upon me.

"Don't you DARE try to down play this!" she shouted, her voice cracking with tears. "You made me marry you. You literally dragged me to that courthouse when I didn't want to. You told me you loved me. Don't act like this is no big deal!"

I couldn't remember the last time I'd been hit, but it definitely wasn't by a woman.

I've never been hit by a female other than Ma.

My hands balling into fists, I breathed in deep and stared her down.

"That is the last time you'll ever lay your hands on me or—"

"Or what," she snapped and hit me again. "It's not like you don't deserve it!"

Then it happened. I lost my composure and grabbed her forearms, shaking her like an out of control toddler.

"Don't fucking touch me again! You're lucky I'm a better man and I don't hit women or I'd–OOOF!!"

For a brief moment, I was seeing stars, the air knocked out of me as her knee came in brutal contact with my dick. The pain brought me to my knees and I collapsed onto the bed, eyes watering, head throbbing.

Two seconds later, she pounced, pummeling me with her fists.

"I hate you, I fucking hate you!" It was like being assaulted by a wild-haired teddy bear. Regaining my wits, I yoked her by the wrists and threw her on the bed, straddling her. She kicked wildly and I used my legs to pin her down, not wanting to risk another injury.

"Let me go! Stop it!"

My reaction could be summed up in one word: pissed. I used my full strength and shook her senseless.

"Listen! Calm the fuck down," I screamed.

"You're hurting me, stop it! Let me go! Help!!"

"Alex, stop it! You're being ridiculous! If you would—OWWWWW! FUCK! SHITTTTT!"

"Sasha, NO!" Alexandria screamed.

Sasha, confused by our antics, bit into my ass with incredible force and pulled me off of her mother. I tried to grab hold of the bed, but she shook me like a rag doll.

"Sasha! Sasha, stop it! Let go of him. Stop! Bad Sasha! Bad!"

Alexandria yanked at her collar while I screamed, trying to beat Sasha off with my fist. Sasha unlocked her jaw and scurried away from me. I jumped to my feet, readying myself for another attack but the movement stretched the bite and a shock of pain hit me like a tank. I let out a litany of curses, hopping around. Alexandria stood in the corner, stroking Sasha's head, calming her. Once Sasha was still, Alexandria moved towards me and I flinched, my arm pulling back, ready to kill just about anyone that came near me; an involuntary reaction. My nuts hurt, my cheek stung, and my ass was bleeding. No one would blame me if I did.

She rolled her eyes and sighed. "Just let me see it."

Begrudgingly, I turned and dropped my pants. She kneeled on the floor to examine the bite and I secretly hoped she'd cup my balls in the process. They could've used a little tenderness.

"You're lucky," she snarled. "It doesn't look deep. You deserved it, though."

She stood and scowled before taking three long strides away from me, crossing her arms over her chest. I pulled my pants back up and sucked in some air through my teeth, my briefs rubbing against the bite.

"I'm going downstairs," I hissed. "I'm gonna let Mia go for the evening. You and that crazy bitch can stay in here until you both calm down."

"Fine! I'd rather be with her anyway," she screamed, throwing something that barely missed my head.

"I was talking to the dog," I screamed and slammed the door behind me. But from the other side, I could hear her breaking down into a hysterical sob.

Damn. What have I done?

Her tears: my Achilles' heel. I hesitated, thinking of all the excuses I could use to walk back into that room, just to try to hold her again, but instead I continued downstairs.

The kids, stunned to silence, stared as I hobbled towards them, my wound throbbing with every step. Mia stood frozen, clutching her cell phone to her chest.

"Did you call the police?" I asked, knowing it was the most logical action for her to take, given the altercation she must have heard.

"No. Not yet."

I snatched the phone away. "I need to go out to the car for a minute. You stay here with the kids, then you can go."

She started to tear up. "She's going to kill me."

"What? This isn't about you," I groaned, annoyed she'd even come to that conclusion.

She sniffed and glanced upstairs. "Well, maybe I should–"

"That is all, Mia!"

I limped out to the car and opened the trunk to find my first aid kit. The moment alone gave me the opportunity to process what the hell had just happened.

How the fuck could she do this?

Fuming, I pulled out my phone and dialed the bitch's number.

"What the hell do you want?" Tiffany snarled.

"Are you happy now," I hissed. "Do you feel accomplished after the bullshit you pulled today?"

"What are you talking about?"

"Did you really feel it necessary to interfere with my life? With my family?"

"What?"

"Don't play stupid!"

"Don't fucking call me stupid! I have no idea what the fuck you're talking about."

"Are you trying to tell me that you didn't call Alex?"

"Who the hell is Alex?" she asked, incredulously. "And whoever he is, why the fuck would I tell him anything about us?"

Him? It took a moment to register. "Are you telling me you never called my wife?"

Silence came over the phone, followed by a chuckle.

"Wait a second, you have some nerve calling me up after you lied about being married, and then accusing me of calling your wife. Until now, I didn't even know her name, how would I have called her? I don't know your house number. I don't even know where you live! All I have is your cell and an email. I'm not that pressed to hire a private detective to find you in some ploy to ruin your life. I could not care less!"

Alexandria's words echoed.

"To accuse is to claim without proof."

"Fine."

Tiffany started yelling but I hung up. She called back five times but I didn't answer. All I could think about as I headed back into the house, preparing to doctor my wound, was Kennedy.

CHAPTER 10

I showed up to the office with a five o'clock shadow, red eyes, and my clothes a wrinkled mess. I looked like shit and every step felt like salt rubbing into my wound. Sharlene's mouth dropped.

"Don't ask."

"O…kay. But… Braxton…"

"Did Clint's people send his contract?" I snapped.

"Well no, but–"

"Fuck! This muther… Get him on the phone now!"

"Yes, but Mr. Braxton? Mr. Paul wants you in his office. Immediately."

Shit… now what?

I dropped my bag in the doorway and limped through the hall, straightening up as soon as I neared Victoria. She smirked, eyes glued on her computer.

"Go on in. He's expecting you," she said, practically singing.

What is she so happy about?

Mr. Paul was at his desk. The moment he saw me he ripped off this glasses and jumped up, waving a piece of paper.

"Braxton! You mind telling me what this is all about?"

I froze, baffled by his unusual temper. "Come again, sir?"

"This letter, addressed to me, came express mail today." He slipped on his glasses and began reading. "'The man you hired, Braxton Earwood, is not the man you think he is. He is a manipulative liar and an adulterer.'"

FUCK!

I swallowed and stood silent. Mr. Paul glanced up, waiting for a reaction, then continued reading. "'He has been splurging on your company dime and fucking… hos…' Braxton? Is this true?"

#8 Unless they got proof, Deny. Deny. Deny.

"Sir, I have no idea what this letter is referring to. That couldn't possibly be—"

"There are pictures, Braxton."

Pictures? Oh shit.

He threw a couple of photos on the desk. I stepped closer, my ass killing me. There were pictures of Tiffany and I at the bar, at the club, in her car, walking into the hotel, walking out of her house... all taken from a distance. I wanted to light his whole desk on fire.

"Sir..."

"All this and you still didn't get that deal inked! Goddamn it, Braxton!"

He slammed his fist on the desk, his face flushed red under his silver hair. I didn't react outwardly, I remained still, but my hands were trembling, ready to punch through a brick wall.

"Look, you don't have to explain anything to me," he added. "I don't give a damn. I've been there. I know how it feels to be caught red handed. It's your business, but this cannot affect MY business. So handle it, keep me out of it, and do your fucking job!"

He threw the letter on the desk and returned to his computer as if I didn't exist. The two-paged typed letter was in large bold face font with no signature; a complete character assassination. I swooped up the evidence against me and stormed out of the room. Victoria wore a huge grin that could have been seen from another state, which meant one thing: she had read the letter, and, no doubt, the entire office knew about it before I had even walked in the door that morning.

As I limped back to my office, every woman in the firm glared at me. They didn't know a thing about Alexandria but sympathized with her, I'm sure, taking out their resentment towards the men that hurt them in the past on me. I'd become the office scapegoat.

Sharlene avoided eye contact and focused on her computer.

"Get me Kennedy Davis on the line. Her number should be in my address book."

"Right away, sir," she mumbled as I slammed my office door shut, the walls vibrating.

Kennedy had a talent for starting trouble between Alexandria and I, but this time she had gone too far. She must have seen me in D.C. with Tiffany. Probably had one of her girlfriends call Alexandria pretending to be Tiffany. She knew where I worked and could have easily sent the anonymous letter.

Never had I seen so much envious backstabbing before in my life. Bitches were just plain cruel to one another without even knowing it.

"Kennedy on line two for you," Sharlene said over the intercom and I snatched up the receiver.

"Kennedy, you stupid mutherfucking bitch! Your lease is up and I want you out of the fucking apartment by the end of this week! I don't care you if have to sleep on the street!"

"What!" she shrieked. "Wait, what the fuck is wrong with you?"

"Like you don't know!"

"You can't just kick me out for no reason!"

"Like hell I can't, you dumb bitch. You didn't even sign a lease. I can do whatever the fuck I want. Pack your shit and be out before I have you dragged out!"

"Wait, Braxton! Why are you coming at me like this? I didn't do nothing," she pleaded.

Such a fucking actress.

"My boss got that little note you sent. Last night I had to sleep in the kid's room after the little shit you pulled with Alex. Do you know she was crying the entire night?"

"Yo, what are you talking about? What's wrong with Alex? What did you do?"

I took a deep breath, trying to calm myself down. She wasn't worth having a heart attack over.

"Hello," she snapped. "Braxton? What's going on?"

"Don't act stupid, Kennedy. The show's over! Why the fuck won't you just leave us alone? I don't want you, I never have. But you're so fucking determine to break up our family"

"I don't know what the fuck you're talking about—"

"Are you happy now? Alex is hurt over a small… indiscretion. She didn't have to know about it—"

"She caught you cheating? How? When? Why didn't she tell me!" She gasped, horrified. "Oh my God! Does she know?! DID YOU TELL HER?!!"

She began to cry, begging me to tell her what happened, genuinely frightened. She really had no idea. Alexandria hadn't told her anything.

But that doesn't make any sense. She tells her everything.

"No," I muttered. "She still doesn't know."

Kennedy sniffled.

"Wait a second," she said, her voice calming down. "She caught you cheating and you think I had something to do with it? HA! You're fucking amazing. How dare you try to take the blame out on me after YOU fucked up! You can't blame anyone else but your damn self."

I glanced up at the portrait of the kids, sitting on the bookcase, my stomach twisting.

Sorry guys. Daddy fucked up.

Sharlene suddenly burst through the door, waving both hands. "I'm sorry to disturb you, sir, but your sister is on line three!"

"My sister?"

My sisters had never called my work number. I doubted they even knew it.

Oh no, Ma!

"Kennedy, I'll call you right back," I said, as my stomach plummeted to my feet.

"What, wait, where's Alex? What did you do…?"

I hung up and switched the line, bracing myself.

"Paris? Paris, what's wrong?" Paris would have been the only one smart enough to call.

"Surprise!" The woman's voice on the other end didn't sound like any of my sisters.

"Who is this?"

"What do you mean who is this?" The woman's giggle was familiar but I couldn't place the voice. Growing agitated, I lost my patience.

"Yo, who the fuck is this? I don't have time for these fucking games!"

"Okay, okay, calm down. It's Rachel."

"Rachel!?" She was the last person I expected to hear from and the last person I wanted to talk to. "What… what the hell do you want? How'd you get this number?"

"I'm not stupid, Braxton, I know how to use Google."

"Okay, you get the gold star for the day," I said, holding the bridge of my nose, fighting a growing headache. "Now what do you want, I'm kinda in the middle of something."

"Oh, okay. I was just wondering if you got my letter."

"Letter?" I opened up my Outlook account. Nothing. I searched around my desk, assuming I had overlooked it.

"There's nothing here. What are you…"

Then it hit me like a bag of bricks thrown in my face. I jumped out of my chair so fast I knocked it over, holding back the urge to scream as the picture became clearer.

"Soooo… how's everything with you?" she said, her voice all cheerful and full of mischief. Rachel was the one following me around like a damn private eye. She was the one who sent the letter to Mr. Paul, with those pictures. And she was the one who called Alexandria, pretending to be Tiffany.

"Why… why did you… just why, Rachel?" I said, exasperated.

"That's exactly what I asked myself when I found out you cheated on me. So how does it feel Braxton, finally being caught?"

I want to fuck this bitch up. I don't even care if she's a woman.

"I wasn't caught. You exposed me," I corrected through clenched teeth. "You took it upon yourself to interfere with matters that had nothing to do with you."

"I had my reasons."

I started to retort but thought against it. She was clearly *non compos mentis*, continuing to argue with her was a waste of time and I refused to give her the satisfaction.

"You're insane, you know that?"

"Well, if I'm crazy it's 'cause you made me this way. You and that bitch! Now she knows how it feels to be cheated on and now you know how it feels to be caught. Soon your Mom will know too since I sent her a little package. Maybe I'll let your kids know, too, someday."

The idea of Rachel coming near my family brought on every murderous thought I'd ever had.

"Rachel," I hissed, too filled with rage to think straight. "I swear, you better not come near me again or I'll–"

"Ha! Braxton, you know you're not going to do anything. And even if you did, I still got the last laugh. I exposed you for the heartless, good for nothing, lying, cheating bastard that you really are. Really, I'm doing *you* a favor. Maybe you'll learn that you can't trick girls into thinking you care about them, that you're their one and only. Tricking them to the point they question their own sanity because of the crazy mind games you play! What did they use to call you, Smooth? Well you ain't so Smooth now, huh?"

I sat back down, trembling in anger, the green monster trying to rip out of my skin.

"You listen to me you fucked up bitch! You come near me or any of my family again I'll put you in a damn body bag myself." I slammed down the receiver and took a deep, calming breath. Rachel. Of all the ghosts of my past, I never thought she would be the one to do so much damage. All the intricate parts of my life were swirling out of control. I struggled to focus, to compose myself before heading down a black hole of darkness, but none of my techniques were working. Sharlene rapped at the door and let herself in.

Now what?

"Not right now, Sharlene. Give me a moment."

"I'm sorry, sir. But Mia is on line one. She said it's urgent!"

Can this day get any worse?

I groaned and snatched up the receiver.

"Yes, Mia. What is Alexandria breaking down about this time?"

"Braxton! Something's happened," she shouted, sounding as if she were outside with dozens of voices around her. A walkie-talkie goes off in the background.

"What do you mean? What's wrong?"

"It's Alex!"

Within seconds I was up on my feet, keys in hand.

"Is she alright? What happened?"

Talk faster, bitch!

"No not that Alex, Lil Alex! The ambulance just left! They're on their way to the hospital."

CHAPTER 11

"I want to be honest with you two," Dr. Helen Chevalier started from the opposite side of a long table in one of the hospital's conference rooms. She was a petite yet round woman, flanked by two surgeons—their faces did not look promising.

"We've all been aware of Alexander's condition and the possibility of complications from the start. The stent we patched on his heart when he was first born was only a Band-Aid, we knew it would eventually have to be replaced as he grew. However, his latest cold has made his heart work a little harder than his body could really handle, expanding the hole."

Alexandria sat as far away from me as possible, without being outside in the parking lot. Her eyes remained focused on the doctors. Trying to concentrate on such an imperative conversation was brutal when we were in the last place in the world I wanted to be. I'd rather stand barefoot on lava than be inside a hospital. The smell made me want to vomit. And now I didn't even have Alexandria to calm me. I dug my nails into the chair to keep myself from running.

"Go on," I urged.

"As of now, Alex is stable, but in critical condition. Surgery is his only chance."

I swallowed, gripping my seat tighter. Alexandria turned pale, her hands shaking, eyes stretched wide. If needles were the apocalypse, I couldn't even fathom her feelings on surgery.

"What type of surgery," I asked, feeling the need to take some type of control of the situation, for Alexandria's sake more than my own.

"Open-heart, same as before. But, his current heart has weakened and we are concerned that he might not survive the surgery."

"Might not??" Alexandria coughed out the words, voice rising with hysteria. "'Might not' survive surgery? Are you saying Alex could die?!"

"We're not betting on that outcome. You're talking to some of the finest surgeons in this country."

Alexandria brought a hand up to her lips, her eyes twitching. A part of me wanted to comfort her. But she hadn't allowed me within two feet of her since Rachel's phone call.

"Will he need a heart transplant?" I said, trying to remain calm. One of us had to.

One of the surgeons chimed in. "We're hoping it won't come to that. We're confident it's repairable. For good this time."

"You didn't answer my question," Alexandria growled, eyes watery. "Are you telling me that my baby could die?"

The doctors squirmed under the pressure, trying to remain professional.

"The only thing that's keeping him alive right now is our machines," Dr. Chevalier admitted. "And his will to live. We're still waiting on a few more images to determine the level of damage. But we want to make sure you know everything upfront."

At that very moment, Alexandria stopped breathing. Neither one of us moved.

"What are his chances, after surgery, with or without a new heart?"

"After recovery, he should be a normal healthy boy."

The words were only somewhat comforting. I took out my phone, prepared to transfer funds out of my savings, willing to pay them whatever they wanted to ensure my boy would be okay. Just to have him healthy and smiling again.

"But a new heart would give him the better chance of survival, correct?" Alexandria asked.

"Yes, but that's not guaranteed," the surgeon said.

"And what's the likelihood that you'll find a heart that is a match in time to save him?" she asked.

The doctors glanced at each other. "We can't say for certain."

Alexandria nodded towards me. "Would his father be a match?"

My head snapped up. Dr. Chevalier frowned, casting a quick, curious look in my direction. The doctors weren't blind to the tension between us.

This fucking woman!

"Alexandria, this isn't time for jokes," I hissed.

"Who's joking?"

I closed my eyes and breathed out slow, refusing to acknowledge her shenanigans. The only thing stopping me from shaking the shit out of her again was thinking of Lil' Alex in that hospital bed.

"He's only eleven months," Alexandria said to them, near tears, and they nodded as if they understood her pain.

"Have we truly exhausted all possibilities?" I asked.

Dr. Chevalier nodded. "We are fully confident, and are determined to ensure Alex has the best quality of life. For a very long time."

After a few more questions, the doctors left us to check on their patients. Alexandria and I sat in silence, the tension of the discussion lingering in the air.

Maybe they're wrong.

They had told us Lil' Alex had died before he was even born. They told me he might not make it through surgery when he was less than an hour old. They told me Alexandria was suffering from internal bleeding, and could possibly die. They told me a lot of shit. Maybe they were wrong again.

Alexandria stood up and walked to the window, gazing at the sunset, still wearing the clothes she wore to the hospital three nights ago: a tattered sweatshirt and stained jeans. Lil Alex had collapsed in his high chair. Alexandria had performed CPR before the ambulance arrived. The thought alone gave me chills; I couldn't imagine what I would've done if I had been there. Other than Ma, I didn't know any woman that would've been strong enough to spring into action like that.

I thought about Lil' Alex's condition and started contemplating where to potentially acquire a heart for Alex. Only illicit options came to mind. I would have to pummel someone, just enough so they were incapacitated, a vegetable. It would need to be someone the world wouldn't miss. Like a bum or crackhead. Kennedy came to mind, but I couldn't live with the thought of my son having that cum-bucket's anything. Then it occurred to me—he'd need an infant's heart. I couldn't go that far.

"I want a divorce," Alexandria said, feigning confidence.

Of course the first words out of her mouth would be idiotic ones.

"That's fine. But it would be an annulment since we haven't been married more than two months."

"Yeah, and in two months you've managed to fuck up completely."

I sighed. I would have rather shot myself in the foot than have this conversation.

"So I want an annulment," she snapped, crossing her arms. "I want the house, the car, and the kids. By the time I get home, I want you out!"

"That's not happening, so you can quit the dramatics. We need to focus on Alex."

She whipped around, her eyes blazing. "Don't tell me what I should be focused on. I'm ALWAYS focused on Alex. I'm ALWAYS focused on my children. What have YOU been focusing on the last couple of weeks?"

I didn't bother countering; it would only exacerbate our argument because she was right. But my pride wouldn't allow me to admit that aloud.

She shook her head. "You're a coward."

The words burned through me until my hands rolled up into fist.

"What did you say?"

"I said, you're a stupid fucking coward," she snapped, her eyes narrowing. "You pretend to be this asshole, then you turn around and do some of the nicest things because that's who you really are. You're a good guy. I know you now, Braxton. I know you want me just as much as I want you. But your stupid fucking pride won't let you admit that. So you'd rather treat me like shit than do what you really want."

My mouth dropped.

When did she start reading minds?

I moved towards her and she flinched away. She might have been right, but I refused to let her hold my head under the guillotine.

"How do you know what I want," I challenged. "You don't even know me!"

"Ha! Then tell me you wanted her as much as you want me!"

"Of course not!"

"Then, WHY! Tell me: why did you do it?" She pleaded. "Tell me why you keep on hurting me!"

The crack in her voice was like bullets to my chest, and I just couldn't lie to her.

"I don't know," I sighed, rubbing my head. "I have no clue. Guess I just did it 'cause I could. But it meant nothing. Why do I have to tell you that? Can't you just see it for yourself, how much I... care about you?"

She scoffed. "Yeah, Braxton. You sleeping with someone else really shows me how much you 'care' about me."

The air quotes made the words sound so trivial.

Why couldn't I just tell her I loved her? What the fuck is my problem?

She rolled her eyes and headed for the door. There was a different type of loathing in her voice, more brutal, cold, and emotionless than ever before. My heart raced, panic sending a jolt up my spine. Could she really be done with me?

"Stop," I said, standing in her way. "Don't be ridiculous, we have to talk!"

"I'm done talking with you," she snapped, passing by me. I yanked her hand back and pulled her into my chest, roping my arms around her.

"Don't," she barked, snatching her hand back. I grabbed her face, crashing my lips into hers, willing her to love me again. Before, this always did the trick, and for a moment, I thought it was working. She dropped her purse, cupping my face and I slammed her against the wall. Our kiss became urgent and desperate, like we were trying to devour one another. But then she pushed against my chest.

"No," she snapped, shoving me away—a stone, once again. I didn't try to force myself on her again. It was clear she couldn't stand me any longer.

"I'll stay at a hotel," I said with a sigh.

Alexandria didn't even look at me as she mumbled, "Good idea."

***

My knee bounced a thousand times a minute as I sat next to Lil' Alex, his breathing ragged, attached to what seemed like hundreds of wires and tubes sustaining him in the children's intensive care unit of Atlanta Medical Center. I kept my back to the door, unable to bare the sights and sounds of the hallway, the sickly children being wheeled in and out. I tried to convince myself that Alex didn't look as bad as those other kids.

After our talk with the doctors, I made calls to several heart specialists around the country. They all agreed with the diagnosis. A risky surgery or bet on a new heart. I stayed up for hours, searching and researching alternatives, looking up potential brain injuries that could leave a person comatose yet keep their heart intact; marginally bothered by the dark ideas swirling in my head. My aversion to hospitals became more intense as the days went on. I threw up twice just watching the nurses charge his IV bag.

I am a God fearing man, Lord. But I would do anything to get him out of this hospital.

So, we gave a go for the surgery, and, after five grueling hours, Lil' Alex was in recovery, but hadn't woken up yet. Dr. Chevalier had said the operation was a success, it was just a matter of how his body would handle it in the days following. This was the worst part, the waiting.

Alexandria practically lived in the hospital with him. She refused to look or even acknowledge my presence. The one time I attempted to start a conversation with her, she looked straight through me as if I was made of glass. Alexandria's mother flew in to help take care of the other kids, and acted as the middleman between us; arranging shifts so we could stay by Alex's bedside. We never wanted him to wake up and not see someone he recognized.

"Come on, little man, wake up," I whispered to him, holding his foot. Every so often I would try talking to him, reading him the sports page, even turning on his favorite cartoon. Nothing.

The door opened and I stood up, expecting Alexandria, but I froze in disbelief at who I saw instead.

"How the fuck did you get here?"

"Bus," Brian said, standing in the doorway. "Ma told me what happened."

Figures.

Brian sat his duffle bag by the door and we stared at each other in silence, neither one of us knowing what to say. He sighed and glanced over at Lil' Alex. "Is this little man?"

"Yeah," I mumbled.

He walked over to the side of the bed, admiring him with a grin. I walked to the other side of the bed, a ball of tense energy, hovering, prepared to kill anyone that hurt my son—including my own brother.

"Damn, he looks a lot like you. You can't really tell by the pictures."

I glanced down at Alex, my little adorable boy, and smiled.

"Nah, he looks more like his mother," I whispered. "You should see Aiden. He's my twin."

Brian laughed. "Well then I don't know what Nina is talking about. Can't deny it, you definitely in there."

He reached out and rubbed Alex's cheek with the back of his fingers. I flinched, my hands itching to slap his away. Brian sucked his teeth and met my eyes.

"Yo, I ain't gonna hurt your son, B. I ain't that much of a fuck up to hurt my own nephew. Chill!"

Damn, had I really been worried Brian would fuck up somehow, pull a wire he wasn't supposed to or something? Yes, he screws up his own life, but I knew deep down Brian wouldn't intentionally hurt anyone, especially family. I shook my head and took a deep breath, nodding as some sort of apology. My nerves were getting the better of me.

"Where's your wife?" he asked, glancing around the room.

"I don't know," I mumbled, rubbing my face. "Somewhere in the hospital. She doesn't like us being in here at the same time."

Brian chuckled. "Man, you must have fucked up big time."

I shrugged, hating Brian for always being so observant.

"How's Ma?" I asked, switching subjects.

"Doing better," he said, pulling up a chair. "She starting to take those pills they prescribed her. I can see a difference. She wanted to come but…"

"Nah, it's better she stay there. Who knows… what will happen."

The guilt bum-rushed me, ripping the words out of my throat. I was unconsciously preparing for the worst. I held Lil' Alex's hand, feeling his warmth. I tried to shake the dark thoughts; but with nothing but the beeping of Alex's monitors filling the room, the cables running into him, the smell of rubbing alcohol, and Brian standing off to the side, watching us, the walls began to close in. Seconds away from losing my shit, Brian cleared his throat and dug into his duffle bag.

"Here," he said and passed me what looked like a brick wrapped in tin foil. "I made this for you. From scratch."

"What is it?"

He grinned. "Just eat it."

I unwrapped the brick and laughed at the pile of moist brownies. Brian always loved to bake, but brownies were his specialty, and were always mixed with weed. He once left a potent batch on the kitchen counter, and unbeknownst to her, Ma ate a couple after coming home from a long shift at work. She was bouncing off the walls for hours. I raised a curious eyebrow at him and he smiled.

"It'll help calm you down. I know how you are about hospitals."

I started to laugh until a woman let out a wretched painful scream in the hallway. I shook my head trying to block out the sound, ready to jump out the window to escape it. Brian quickly closed the door.

"Hey, I know you think you all classy and better than everyone and shit, but you ain't fooling me. Eat a fucking brownie, man! You need it."

Brian knew me better than most, and knew I wouldn't last another day in this place if I didn't pull it together. Relenting, I picked up a slice and chewed on the chocolaty treat.

Brian smirked. "Don't eat too much, don't want you to fall off the wagon."

"These are pretty good," I said between bites. Better than I remembered.

"They had me in the kitchen. I'm like a chef now. Taking after Ma."

"You know, I know a dude opening up a lounge back home. I can talk to him, see if he needs any help in the kitchen."

Brian smiled with a sheepish shrug. "That'd be cool."

We sat in silence, staring at Alex, while the weed raced through my blood system, slowing down my heartbeat. My nerves began to ease, muscles loosening around the bones.

Damn, I forgot what this was like.

A weird sense of peace and clarity melted into me. For the first time, I sat in the hospital room with my son without feeling the need to jump out the window. I touched his little leg, hoping to spark a reaction. He continued to sleep.

Brian gaped at the monitors surrounding Alex like he was watching a football game.

"Thanks for this," I said, hinting at the brownies.

"No sweat."

"Does your parole officer know you're here?"

He grinned. "I wouldn't worry about all that. Oh yeah, got something else for ya, too."

He dug into his bag and pulled out a manila envelope, addressed to Ma with Rachel's name in the return address. I stared at Brian.

How did he know!

"Ma never saw it," he said. "I'm sure you never want her to either."

"But, why? You never even met her."

He shrugged. "I heard the name enough. And I know you two didn't leave on speaking terms. So I thought to myself, why the hell is she sending Ma anything?"

I shook my head. "Thanks, man."

He laughed. "Damn, bitches be wildin' out over you."

"That's not exactly a good thing anymore," I sighed and threw the envelope in the trash, then yanked it back out.

If Alexandria found these in here she'd fucking kill me.

Brian laughed. "Let me ask you something. Back when we were kids, you changed, big time? Why?"

I shrugged. "We all have to grow up sometime."

"Nah, not like that. You straight flipped, like overnight. No warning, no nothing. What happened? That's all I want to know."

I sighed, and wrapped up the rest of the brownies.

"Remember, that night you got popped for that robbery and the cops came by and picked you up? The same night Regal died?"

Brian swallowed. "Yeah."

"When I got home that night, I heard Ma crying in the living room. That's all it took."

"Nah, yo," Brian said, rubbing his head. "You were hearing things. Ma never cries."

"I heard her. She broke down right in Pop's chair. I guess she didn't know I was home."

Brian shook his head. "Damn."

"So that's all it took. I heard Ma crying. Regal was gone. You were in jail. So I went to school the next day and asked how I could get into college."

"Smart," Brian relented. "You were always mad smart. Sometimes, I wished I would have followed some of that shit Regal was spitting. Maybe I wouldn't be where I'm at now."

"Nah. You were right. I was being an asshole. Still am."

He gave me a once over. "You look like shit."

"Thanks. I've been up all night."

"Why don't you go home, get some rest, see your kids." He laughed. "Yo, I can't believe you got four of them!"

"I can't either," I chuckled.

"But I always knew you were going to be like this, married with kids. It's a good look on you. You were always so overprotective of us. Anyone that wasn't your family, your blood, you didn't give a shit about. You were more of a father figure to the girls, and more of a husband to Ma, than Pops ever was." He sighed.

My thoughts drifted toward Alexandria and the kids.

Brian tapped my arm. "Man, go home. I got this!"

The offer sounded enticing but what if Alex woke up? He didn't know Brian, and in some ways, I wasn't sure who Brian really was anymore, either.

#2 Trust no one.

I shook my head. "I don't know."

"Don't worry. If your wifey comes through, I'll explain you went home to take a shower or something. I won't leave little man alone. You can trust me."

I did trust Brian. More than I trusted anyone. He and I both held the same regard when it came to family.

"Aight man. Just don't leave him. If anything happens, even if he only moves an inch, call."

"Cool."

I stood over Lil' Alex, trying to convince myself it was safe to leave him. Wishing he would just wake up and smile at me. I remembered his first smile, at bath time, when he was only a couple of weeks old. Sponging him off in his little basin, he looked up and gave me a gummy grin. Every part of me defrosted and I couldn't stop smiling back at him. I don't think I ever smiled so much in my entire life.

How did I ever live without him?

I rubbed his hand. "I'll be back in a little while, buddy," and started towards the door when Brian said something under his breath.

"What was that?" I asked.

"I said, I'm sorry," he repeated, without looking at me. "I didn't know they were going to retaliate and shoot up Ma's house like that. I thank God every day that she wasn't home. I would have never forgiven myself if anything had happened to her. I don't know what I'd do without her. I love her just as much as you do, B. I wish you'd see that. And I wish you'd see that I'm trying to change my life around." He glanced over his shoulder. "I ain't trying to go back to prison, you understand?" He turned back to Alex as if I had already left the room, holding his hand. "It's alright, little man. Uncle B is here."

I stood frozen in the door, watching him talk to my son. The truth: I had admired Brian. No matter his transgressions, he was there for me when we were growing up, he never held back punches or backed down. He was honest, humble, and brave. He took an almost fifteen-hour bus ride from Boston just to apologize.

And I couldn't even apologize to Alexandria when I knew I was dead wrong.

***

The sun was setting as I tiptoed into the house and snuck upstairs. It had only been a few weeks and I felt like a visitor in a place I was still paying a mortgage on. But the smell beat the unfamiliarity of my hotel room. The kids were in the kitchen with Mia and Mrs. Stone, rolling around in their walkers, giggling. It was unfair to them, but I didn't have the energy to play. Even on the drive over, I swerved a few times, drifting in and out of sleep. The weed made my whole body slow down and relax.

The bedroom was still a catastrophe, clothes and sheets thrown everywhere, curtains askew. In desperate need of a power nap, I kicked off my shoes, threw my sweaty shirt in the pile on the floor, and slipped on a pair of sweat pants. I still had mixed feelings about leaving Brian alone with Lil' Alex, but I had to trust him. Deep down, I knew he wouldn't disappoint.

I'll just take an hour nap and head back to the hospital.

As I started to make the bed, the door opened behind me.

"What are you doing here?"

Alexandria stood in the doorway, skin damp, snuggled in a large orange towel. Her drenched hair slicked back, dripping on the floor. She smelled like her citrusy hair products.

Stunned, I stuttered to find the right words.

"I…"

"You're supposed to be at the hospital with Alex," she screamed, frantic. "What happened? Is he okay?"

She stormed towards me, her eyes wide, clutching the towel to her chest as if bracing for impact.

"He's okay. My brother is at the hospital with him."

She blinked a couple of times at first, dissatisfied with my answer, but then exhaled, hanging her head low.

"Oh God, I thought…"

Our eyes met as she cut off her own thought and plopped down on the bed, her chocolate eyes focused on the floor. She breathed in through her nose a couple of times to slow herself down. It reminded me of that Lamaze class we took. Unsure of what to do, I closed the door, I assumed she'd want me to leave, but I waited to make sure she didn't pass out in shock, first. Her hair dripped down her face and her once lustful, adoring eyes were void, drained of all emotion. The room seemed smaller, the air between us tense but calm.

"Do you want me to leave?" I asked, knowing damn well I wasn't leaving until I knew for certain she was okay.

"I don't care what you do," she sighed, her voice horse and scratchy. Her eyes were back on the floor, starring at nothing.

"I'm surprised you're home."

She paused for a beat. "A nurse was kind enough to inform me that I smelled. I haven't had a shower in three days. I figured I would take a quick one before heading back." I hadn't seen her look so weak and pale since she was pregnant. I shuddered, remembering her condition during those last few weeks on bed rest. I rummaged through a few ideas, trying to figure out what to say next, or how to fix her.

"Did you eat?"

She didn't respond; her eyes still glued to the floor. Parents don't typically acknowledge any one child as their favorite, but we both knew Lil' Alex was hers. They had an unmistakable bond. She knew him before he was even born and nursed him back to health with extreme diligence. But she wouldn't be able to take care of him while being a zombie. Alex needed her.

I needed her.

I headed to the kitchen and took out a loaf of bread, mayo, smoked turkey, and swiss cheese slices from the fridge. Mrs. Stone and Mia stared in awe, but said nothing. The kids stretched their little hands, whimpering and reaching for me but I focused on the sandwich. I couldn't play with them, not just yet.

I'll just take care of her. Everything will be back to normal. She'll forgive me. She always does. She just needs to relax for a little while.

That's when I remembered Brian's brownies and grabbed them on the way upstairs with a perfect turkey sandwich and a bottle of water.

Alexandria hadn't moved, her body frozen, hair curling as it dried. The sandwich in hand, I debated whether I should feed her myself. Instead, I pushed the plate in her eyesight.

"Eat." She didn't even look at it. "Eat," I repeated, offering her the plate again. She remained still.

"Alexandria, you have to eat. You have to keep your strength up."

"He's gonna die. I... can't watch him die. Not again. I can't." Her voice quivered as the tears welled up.

I exhaled slow, fighting the urge to slap some sense into her.

"Don't say that. He is not gonna die. He will be fine. Eat."

She shook her head. "My little football. I can't watch him die... I can't... I'm so scared."

The thought of Lil' Alex; tubes attached, monitors surrounding him, in his coma-induced sleep...

My son.

Determined to hold it together, I shook the thoughts away and held my ground.

"He. Is. Not. Going. To. Die. EAT!" The tone in my voice caught her attention. She glanced up, her eyes narrowing to a stinging glare with profound rage.

"I hate you," she said with utter conviction.

"That's fine. Eat."

"Fuck you," she said, revolted by the sandwich.

Frustrated, I slammed the plate on the nightstand and grabbed a half. "Alexandria, eat the god damn sandwich!" For a moment, we looked like Ike and Tina Turner, fighting over a slice a cake as I tried to force the sandwich down her throat. She pushed me away, turning her face up as if I was offering her Sasha's Alpo. I tried again and she struck the sandwich out of my hands. Before I could react, she attacked me, wildly wailing her fist against my chest, her wet hair slapping me as I tried to contain her fit.

"Get away from me," she screamed.

"Stop, Alex, STOP!"

But she didn't. We were once again fighting on the bed, but this time, it felt as if she was looking for anything to hit. Her rage wasn't directed at me, it was directed at the world. I thought of Lil' Alex and remained calm, letting her take out as much anger as she needed to, turning into her punching bag.

My son needs his mother. I need her. I can't do this without her.

I held her tight, containing her struggle, but she didn't relent. She continued to curse, slap, hit, and punch me until her tense body trembled. She let out an ear piercing scream, like a demon flying out of her belly, muffled by my chest. She went limp under my arms and stopped struggling—spent.

As I held her to my chest, never wanting to let her go, she sobbed in anguish. It was my fault she was in such a state. If I hadn't strayed, we would've been working together to help Alex. We would've been strong together. Instead, we were street brawling while my son hung on to life.

"I'm sorry," I said into her hair, her arms clutched around my neck. "Baby, I'm sorry for everything. I'm so sorry."

I rolled to my side without losing hold of her, stroking her hair, cuddling her in my arms. She started to simmer, her sobs dwindling down to a whimper. We lay stiff until the room went black with the night. Her eyes were still wide and anxious, staring at nothingness. There wasn't another time that I could remember just sitting still; the two of us holding each other. It felt good. It felt right. The drama with Rachel, Tiffany, Kennedy, even Brian was trivial. And as much as I pretended not to care about her, she needed to be my one and only concern. Life would have been so much simpler if I had just focused on her.

If she'd only let me take care of her...

I sat up and leaned against the headboard, positioning her between my legs, leaning her back against my chest. She was like a lifeless doll as I moved her around. I kissed the top of her head and rubbed her arms, erasing the goose bumps that riddled them. I brought the remaining half of the sandwich to her lips. She hesitated, then took a small bite, chewing slowly.

After she finished the sandwich, I gave her a piece of the brownie. She ate it and grabbed another slice. I wasn't into drugging girls so they'd stay with me, but desperate times called for desperate measures. I ate another two slices with her.

Thank you, Brian.

When she finished her third slice, we sat silently in the dark, listening to the kids play downstairs, banging on their toys, giggling. They were happy, but still, it didn't feel right. There was a gapping void in the house with Lil' Alex missing.

Dr. Chevalier's words echoed in my head over and over again, haunting me. The muscles in my back started to tense, thinking of how our family would forever be changed. We would have one extra highchair, car seat, crib, walker, and an empty space in our stroller, a painful reminder of his loss. I tried to remain poised but the pain ambushed me. I was beginning to feel the fear that Alexandria was experiencing all along, a black shadow covering the thoughts of the future.

What would our everyday life be like without him? How would we recover?

Our family wouldn't be the same if we lost Lil' Alex. We as parents would never be the same. I couldn't do anything to save him or comfort him. All I could do is wait. And what about Alexandria, would she ever forgive me? Everything in my life was out of my control and I was powerless.

I'd only cried once in my life: the day I lost Regal. So maybe it was the weed, but all my choked up emotions came spewing out.

Alexandria tilted her head up. "Are you crying?"

I sniffed and wiped my eyes. "No."

She stared, then quickly spun around, straddling me. "Don't do that. Don't lie to me anymore. For once, be honest and tell me what you're really thinking."

I swallowed and cupped her face, staring into her beautiful eyes. The weed made it easy to blurt out everything I was feeling.

"Honestly, I'm scared. I'm scared of losing Alex and I'm scared of losing you. I'm scared of losing my family." I breathed in deep. "I love you Alexandria. I want you. I've always wanted you."

She nodded. "I know."

"You know," I chuckled. "Cocky much?"

She didn't even crack a smile. "Braxton, deep down, you're a good guy, I know you are. But what I don't understand is why you act like this. Why are you so mean? *Why* do you treat me this way?"

I was so exhausted that the truth just seemed so much easier than following any of my rules. "You left."

She blinked twice. "Huh?"

"I wanted to be with you. And you left. You left me."

She searched my face in disbelief, her mouth dropping. "I… I didn't know you felt that way." She combed the hair out of her face. "I just don't get it. That last night… why didn't you say something? *Anything.*"

"Because, I'm not some super-mushy-lovey-dovey guy," I said, rolling my eyes. "And I'm never going to be. But, I can tell you that I love the way you smell, your laugh, your giggle, your smile, your neck. I love the way you take care of me, even when I don't want you to. I love the way you take care of the kids. I love the feeling when I'm inside you, I love the look on your face when you come, and I love that I'm the one, the only one, that's put that look there. I can't think of anyone else in this world I want to be with more than you."

She bit her lip. "So the way you are… or the way you treat me… what is it, like, left over resentment? You're still mad at me for leaving you?"

"Probably, yes," I said with a groan. "You're the one part in my life I have no control over, but what I want the most. It's fucking frustrating."

She chuckled. "Thanks. I try."

It felt so good to see her smile that I started grinning myself.

"I have to ask you something." I swallowed, feeling the tension pulsing in my ears, nervous for a change. "If I had asked you to stay… with me. Would you have stayed?"

She held her breath for a few seconds before biting her lip again.

"I don't know," she said with a shrug. "We had …issues. Plus, I still needed to live my life. Take a chance for my career. And I don't regret it. But if you had asked me, if I had known how you felt… I would have found a way to make it work."

I smiled. "That's fair. I expected nothing less from you. You've always been fiercely independent. You never really needed me."

"That's not true," she said, curling a hand around my cheek. "I've always needed you, even if I didn't say it. I need you now."

Damn, it feels good to hear that.

"Alex will be fine," I said, giving her a soft kiss. She nodded, eyes full of tears again and cuddled into my chest. I stroked her hair like I was petting Sasha. After a few minutes, her eyes glazed over, staring into the unknown, high as a kite. But she didn't look happy or any less tense.

Still over-thinking.

She needed a distraction and so did I.

My hands made their way down her neck, massaging her shoulders. I kissed her ear and she didn't move. My fingers trickled down her breast, down her stomach, until they reached their intended destination, my favorite spot, right inside her. She shifted and closed her eyes, letting me in deeper. Gently, I rolled her off my lap and snuggled on top of her, brushing the hair out of her face. Even in the low light, she was exquisite.

It was more of a need than a desire, I needed to be inside her. I unwrapped her towel like a delicate present I didn't want to break. Her eyes rolled back as I sucked on her nipple, kissing down her stomach, but she remained unmoved. Finally, just as my face snuggled in between her thighs, her hand touched the top of my shoulder. I froze and our eyes locked.

"I won't have sex with you until you get tested. I don't trust you or the bitch you fucked."

Well, she's high but she's not stupid.

I sighed and nodded, with the full intention of still digging her out, until the phone rang. I'd never seen her eyes grow so big, paralyzed with fear. I jumped up, bracing myself. She grabbed my hand with a squeeze, and I answered the call.

"Yo! He's awake," Brian laughed on the other end. "Hey, little man, say hi to your Daddy!"

CHAPTER 12

Six months later…

"Of course I love it! It's just really fancy for today, that's all."

With an uneasy smile, Alexandria fiddled with the straps on the white sundress I bought from some store in New York she loved. Her long hair pushed away from her face with a navy blue headband.

"I thought you'd approve," I said, dressed in a navy blue suit and a crisp white button down shirt.

"I do, I do! Just don't know why I couldn't wear the dress I bought. Everyone else has on blue. And your Mother must think I'm a heathen, wearing a sleeveless dress to church."

I chuckled, working my way closer to her.

"I know you're not worried about being a sinner after what we did this morning," I whispered in her ear, easing my hand down her back. Grinning, she punched my arm, her face growing red. Images of us fucking in the shower, then on the sink, then on the bathroom door popped into my head.

"Cut it out," she said, distracted by the heap of toddlers at our legs, pulling at her arm. It still fascinated me, seeing them walk, even run, without assistance. I almost miss carrying them everywhere.

"Ma, Ma," Aiden said, no longer struggling with the word.

"Yes, baby," she laughed, rubbing his head as he latched on to her leg.

"Okay, guys, smile for the picture," Kennedy said—for once dressed as modest as she could muster.

Bethany, Brandi, Aiden, and Lil' Alex stood wobbling on the front steps of the church in their all white jumpers and dresses, wincing a smile underneath the blinding hot sun. I hated when the kids were dressed alike, but today I didn't mind.

Kennedy snapped a couple of photos and smiled. "That's my fun bunch right there!"

The kids shrieked and giggled, running towards her. All except Lil Alex. I held his hand to keep him from straining himself. He looked up at me with his mother's scowl.

"Take your time," I warned. Even if he did make a full recovery, just as the doctors predicted, I didn't take open-heart surgery lightly. He would have to become accustomed to my over-protectiveness.

"Jeez, let him live a little," Alexandria said with a devilish grin. She replaced Lil' Alex's hand with her own, intertwining our fingers, as he ran off to play. I had turned into her: a proverbial worrywart. It was disgusting.

The parking lot of the church was full of our family, everyone in town to help celebrate the kids' christening. My sisters chatted with Alexandria's cousins and my aunts laughed with my co-workers. The two uncles, Alexandria's brother Chris and my brother Brian stood on the side lines.

Even Clint, my new client, made it down with his very pregnant wife-to-be. As soon as I had made the decision to be his manager, several other athletes approached me. By the end of the year, I would be leaving Etose Firm to start my own, just as Clint suggested.

"They look so adorable," Alexandria said, watching the kids play. "We should take a picture. Let me borrow your phone, it has the better camera."

"I left it in the car."

"What? Why? You never leave your phone. Ever!"

I shrugged and pulled her closer, kissing her temple. "Everyone I need to talk to is right here."

She smiled, blushing.

"Ok, we're ready!" Ma said from the top of the church steps, dressed in a floral blue dress and standing beside the pastor. "Come on in!"

While we focused on Lil' Alex's recovery and subsequent therapy, Ma continued to plan the kids' christening. Alexandria was grateful to pass on the task. The house was decorated and ready for a reception with over a hundred people. Ma was glowing, healthy, and almost back to normal herself. She even put some weight back on—with the help of Brian's cooking. He was enrolled in culinary school, which I was happily paying for.

The extended family walked into the church first, taking their seats, as Alexandria and I held the kids' hands, leading them inside. The church smelled like damp wood and echoed under our footsteps. The kids, confused by all the attention, became silent, amazed by the high ceilings and stain glass windows. It didn't occur to me that it was their first time in a church, ever.

Damn, we need to take them more often.

I glanced at Alexandria, who was also observing their fascination. We locked eyes and she nodded in agreement, both of us having the same thought. We were like that more than ever these days, in each other's head, moving as one unit. How it always should have been.

The pastor waited at the altar. We exchanged greetings as the kids, still lost in amazement, gazed with curious wonder before he began his service— that lasted all of five minutes, though, since keeping them still was close to impossible. The godparents, Kennedy and Brian, stood on either side of us, helping to corral the kids as Pastor Durum anointed their heads. Bethany fussed at the water trickled on her, swatting his hand away, while Lil' Alex seemed at peace with his surroundings. Alexandria teared up and kissed the top of his head. Just as Pastor Durum was about to wrap up, I took the opportunity to interrupt.

"Uh… Pastor Durum. One small request."

Alexandria's head snapped, mortified. "What is wrong with you?" she grumbled, throwing daggers with her eyes while the family behind us in the pews mumbled.

"Just a small favor to ask." I said, grinning at her.

Killing two birds with one stone…

"Sure, Braxton," Pastor Durum said with a smile, playing along.

"Well, since we're all here, I don't suppose you could marry us while you're at it?"

"What he means is, can they get the two for one special," Brian added.

The pew erupted with cheer as Pastor Durum laughed. Alexandria's mouth dropped with a gasp, mimicking the kids' confusion. Then she glanced down at her dress.

"You planned this?"

I shrugged and she turned to Kennedy, shaking her head in shock.

"Calm down, it's okay," Kennedy laughed as she fixed Alexandria's hair and reapplied some lip-gloss.

Brian stepped up and I handed over Brandi and Aiden.

"My best man?" I offered.

"Of course," Brian said, smiling, and in a surprising move, one that even shocked Ma, he hugged me. "I'm proud of you, B. Always have been."

I clapped his back. "Proud of you, too," I whispered.

We glanced at Alexandria, still stuttering in disbelief. He stepped to the side with the kids, laughing. Mrs. Stone rushed over to hug her. She hugged her back with rigid arms.

"But… But, I…"

Ma scooped Bethany up on her hip as Mrs. Stone scooped up Lil' Alex.

"Ok, now. Remember to breathe," Kennedy said to Alexandria before raising a "Don't fuck this up," eyebrow at me. I nodded in agreement and locked eyes with Alexandria. Stunning and radiant, just like the day I met her.

"I just don't…" she mumbled, eyes wide, petrified. I took both her hands, rubbing circles with my thumbs in her palms.

Wow. I'm really going to do this.

"Are you ready?" Pastor Durum asked. I gave him a resounding nod of approval. "Okay, let us–"

"Wait!" Alexandria yipped, attempting to jerk her hands away. "We don't need to get married. You don't have to do this. It's just a piece a paper!"

"Alex, I…"

"I'm happy with the life we have. But IF we do this, for real this time, there's no turning back. 'Till death do us part, and all that shi—stuff! We'll be like a gang—blood in, blood out."

Our families roared with laughter and Brian leaned over my shoulder. "By the way, I really like her."

Alexandria bit her lower lip, staring at her feet as her cheeks flushed. I cradled her cheek to grab her attention. She had her doubts and I didn't fault her for them. But I gave a reassuring nod.

This is what I want.

Her eyes softened, regaining their normal shape and she closed her gaping mouth, shaking away whatever black thoughts were creeping into her head.

"We're ready," I said to Pastor Durum.

As he began the service, I focused only on Alexandria, glowing like she had ingested stars. There was no one in the world like her, and I was ready, willing, and able to marry her. A true marriage, not one out of convenience, or necessity, but out of love.

"Braxton, do you take Ms. Alexandria Stone, as your lawfully wedded wife, forsaking all others, to have and to hold, for richer or poorer, in sickness and in health, till death do you part?"

Alexandria's eyes bulge at the "forsaking" part and gulped.

"There's no one I want more," I said firmly. "I do"

Alexandria exhaled, her shoulders easing.

"Alexandria, do you take Mr. Braxton Earwood as your lawfully wedded husband, forsaking all others, to have and to hold, for richer or poorer, in sickness and in health, till death do you part?"

She grinned and snatched her hands away. My stomach dropped.

What the fuck?

She raced around the altar, collecting our children, bringing them closer. They surrounded her, still confused yet captivated, their little hands clutching her dress. She scooped Lil' Alex on her hip and turned to me with a glorious smile.

"WE do!"

There was an "awww" from the pews as I laughed, looking down at their bright bubbly faces. There they were, Alexandria plus four, the loves of my life, all staring at me; happy and most of all healthy, my unexpected joys. My family.

#1 Family, above everything.

Brandi and Aiden wrapped themselves around my legs giggling and I lifted Bethany on to my shoulders.

"The rings please," Father Durum said to Brian and Kennedy. "Please place the rings on each other's fingers and say 'with this ring, I thee wed.'"

"With this ring, I thee wed," I said, placing the engagement ring on her finger. The one I wanted to give her months ago. She mouthed a "whoa," staring at the blinding rock, almost dropping Lil' Alex.

"Alex," Kennedy said poking her back again. She passed her my ring and with her one free hand, she slipped it on my finger.

"With this ring, I thee wed."

Alexandria took another moment to stare at her ring and mouthed another, "Whoa."

"By the power vested in me, I now pronounce you: husband and wife. You may kiss your bride!"

With the kids still strapped to us like monkeys, I leaned over and kissed her; a tender, gentle kiss. Not as lustful and passionate as our first quickie wedding, but the sparks still ignited a flame that consumed me. If I could kiss her like this forever, I would.

Fuck, I love this woman.

The church exploded with applause, and the kids joined in, happy for any opportunity to clap. I wrapped an arm around her waist, hugging her close.

"I promised you a ring, didn't I?" I whispered in her ear.

She pulled away and rolled her eyes.

"Ugh! It's disgusting how much I love you."

I chuckled. "I love you, too."

Her cheeks grew red as we gazed at each other, the world around us quieting. Suddenly, I didn't want to be in church any longer or with our families. I didn't want to share her—never have. I just wanted it to be us. Alone in our own little world, just the way I liked it.

But Kennedy jumped over to embrace her best friend.

"Oh my God, Alex, I can't believe… damn! Look at that rock!"

"Please, Ken," Alexandria said with a grin. "Call me MRS. Earwood!"

I laughed and took her hand.

That doesn't sound too bad.

THE RULES

#1 Family, above everything
#2 Trust no one.
#3 Never let them see you sweat.
#4 Treat everything like a business. Even love.
#5 Speak intelligently. It throws victims off.
#6 Never raise your voice. The loudest one in the room is the dumbest.
#7 Think three steps ahead in all situations.
#8 Unless they got proof, Deny. Deny. Deny.
#9 Never catch yourself in a bad situation twice.
#10 Stay fresh and clean.
#11 Cut dead weight quick.
#12 Be better than the first and the last.
#13 Never let a man or woman hold anything over you.

ACKNOWLEDGEMENT

First, my same thank yous apply from the last book, but now I'd like to thank EVERYBODY that supported MISCONCEPTIONS. Like everybody—from co-workers to my Pastor, to every single one of you that left a review on Amazon. A special shout out to Eb and Monee who threw me an awesome book release party, something I couldn't have done myself. I wasn't expecting such amazing feedback and I am truly grateful! I'm sorry this new book took so long. You know…life happens.

Second, I'd like to thank my Parental Unit (Mother and Daddy, that's their nickname) for supporting me by spreading the word, selling books to their friends, and watching my dog-child while I traveled the world!

Third, thanks Jessica, Artesia, Janet, Panama, Kathy, Christine, Robin, and a whole slew of Twitter followers who love and I mean LOVE Alex and Bad Habit.

Shout out to Raquel for editing BAD HABIT and dealing with my mini melt downs throughout the year.

My support system rocks.

About The Author

Blu Daniels is a TV professional by day, novelist by night, awkward black girl 24/7. A Howard University graduate and Brooklyn native, she is a lover of naps, cookie dough, beaches, and glamorously nerdy stuff. She currently resides in BK with her adorable Chihuahua, Oscar, working on her next novel.

Follow her on twitter *@BluDaniels*

Learn more at:
http://bludaniels.blogspot.com
http://writeinbk.com

Coming Soon*

More Misconceptions

Miss Alex? She misses you too!

Five years after her miraculous pregnancy, Alexandria is BACK, juggling a spunky set of quadruplet kindergartners, embracing her new role in the Atlanta elite, and still struggling yet loving her Bad Habit. But when tragedy strikes, Alex will make decisions that will push their relationship to the edge of no return. Can they survive another betrayal?

Hilarious and sexy as ever, MORE MISCONCEPTIONS reunites Alex and Braxton one last time to see what their love can overcome.

*Want to know when this book drops? Sign up for my *newsletter*. I promise, it'll be painless!